THE EGYPTIAN
ANTIQUITIES MURDER

THE EGYPTIAN
ANTIQUITIES MURDER

SARA ROSETT

THE EGYPTIAN ANTIQUITIES MURDER

Book Three in the High Society Lady Detective series

Published by McGuffin Ink

ISBN: 978-0-9988431-8-6

Copyright © 2019 by Sara Rosett

Cover Design: Alchemy Book Covers

Editing: Historical Editorial

Map Illustration by L. Rosett

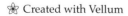 Created with Vellum

ACKNOWLEDGMENTS

To my writing buddies, Jami and Danielle,
and
my faithful Patreon supporters,

Carol S. Bisig
Margaret Hulse
Connie Hartquist Jacobs
Carolyn Schrader

A NOTE ABOUT TITLES AND SURNAMES

Peers in Britain are addressed and known by their title, but the title is often different from the family surname. Thus, the fictional Lord Mulvern in *The Egyptian Antiquities* Murder is addressed as "Lord Mulvern," but his given name is Lawrence Curtis. His niece Agnes has the courtesy title of Lady Agnes because her father was also a peer, but her given name (and the name she signs her correspondence with) is "Agnes Curtis."

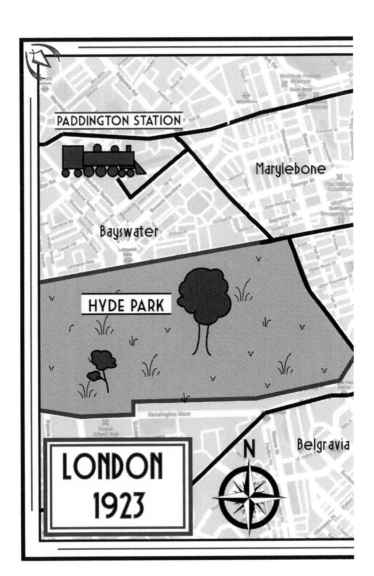

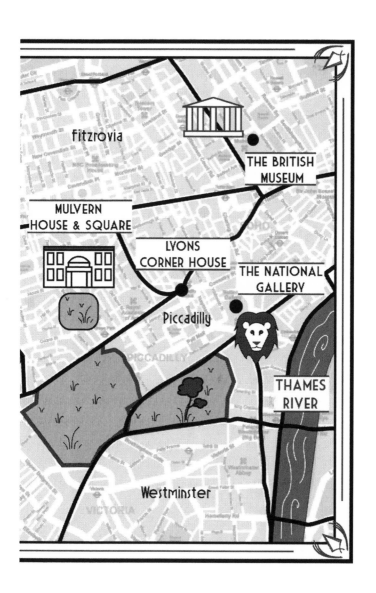

Fitzrovia

THE BRITISH
MUSEUM

MULVERN
HOUSE & SQUARE

LYONS
CORNER HOUSE

THE NATIONAL
GALLERY

Piccadilly

THAMES
RIVER

Westminster

CHAPTER ONE

October, 1923

*E*ven on a drizzly autumn day, Mulvern House didn't look as if a mummy's curse hung over it. Set back from the road, behind a wall of peaked wrought-iron fencing and surrounded with swaths of lawn and lush plantings, the Mayfair town house seemed solid and respectably elegant. Beyond the semicircular sweep of the drive, its three stories rose in symmetrical Georgian sophistication.

I paused at the open gates and checked my wristwatch. A quarter to ten. I was early, which showed how nervous I was. I wasn't normally someone who arrived at appointments fifteen minutes beforehand, but I was meeting with Lady Agnes Mulvern. I didn't want to put a foot wrong. Arriving too early was out of the question.

I walked past the open gates and strolled through the exclusive neighborhood around the fenced park at the center of Mulvern Square. The drizzle was light, and with my warm felt cloche I didn't need to put up my umbrella. A wind with a sharp edge pulled at my skirt, and I gathered the lapels of my new wool coat around my neck. Within a few blocks, I left the residential area and joined the quick pace of Mayfair shoppers on a commercial street.

I had the letter I'd received from Lady Agnes tucked away in my handbag, but I didn't need to take it out to read it again. I knew the short missive by heart. Lady Agnes and her family were having trouble with some nasty rumors about their uncle's death. A mutual friend, Sebastian Blakely, had recommended Lady Agnes contact me. I'd helped sort out an unpleasant situation during a party at Sebastian's country home, and I was pleased he'd mentioned me to Lady Agnes.

The fact she'd contacted me on Sebastian's recommendation meant I might actually be able to make my own way in the world. I was a well-read woman with an education befitting a lady—I had the ability to carry on a conversation about the weather for at least a quarter of an hour, and I could sort out complex seating arrangements at a dinner party—but neither my lady-like education nor my status as a gentlewoman had been advantageous when it came to finding paid employment. Instead of working for a company or individual, I'd had to create my own job.

I'd done fairly well in the line of work I'd fallen into, which was helping people handle sensitive matters discreetly. I'd successfully completed the two jobs I'd taken on. I'd made some headway in supporting myself, but my money troubles were far from over. I felt as if I'd dragged myself up to a narrow ledge where I was balanced precariously. Any misstep could send me plummeting back into the mass of the unemployed. If I could convince Lady Agnes to hire me, then solve her problem, I could really be on my way. There's nothing like a recommendation from the aristocracy to boost a commercial concern.

A high-pitched voice drew my attention as I reached the end of the street. A newspaper boy in a flat cap called out, "Mummy haunts Mayfair town house. Details inside. Get your copy right here." I handed over a few coins and took a newspaper. It wasn't one of the staid, respectable papers. The newssheet was *The Hullabaloo*, one of the tabloids that specialized in scandalous headlines in gigantic fonts.

The story was front and center, above the fold. I checked the byline, but it was a man's name, not my boarding-school chum Essie Matthews, who worked for the newspaper. A picture of the new Lord Mulvern, Gilbert, Lady Agnes's brother, ran alongside the text, which described a maid—unnamed, of course—who recounted horrible wailing sounds emanating from the great gallery in Mulvern House.

"No one wants to go in there," the scandal sheet quoted the unnamed servant. According to the story, the last housemaid who had dusted in the great gallery fainted and had to be carried out by two footmen. Once she came around, she refused to return to work and left her position, choosing instead to go back to her family in the country. The article included a statement from a current resident of Mulvern House—also unnamed—

3

who said, "No one will go into the great gallery now. The doors are chained shut to keep the spirit locked in."

I skimmed to the last lines. "The troubles continue for the family of the late Lord Mulvern, eminent Egyptologist and possessor of a cache of mummies. Will the Curtis family ever be free of the torment?"

A church bell rang out, and I started. It was the first of several chimes. The quarter of an hour was over. It was ten o'clock, the moment I should have been knocking on the door of Mulvern House. I thrust the newspaper at the boy. I certainly couldn't carry it into Mulvern house.

"Don't you want it, lady?"

"No, you can have it back. It's not even creased."

He shrugged and returned it to his stack as I dashed back the way I'd come. I reached Mulvern Square in a few minutes and sped through the gates, along the curve of the drive, and up the steps to the porte-cochère. I was only slightly breathless when a butler with a head of abundant gray hair opened the door. I informed him I had an appointment with Lady Agnes. A footman took my damp coat, and the butler said, "Lady Agnes is in the morning room. Please follow me."

He had remarkable speed for his age, and I hurried to keep up. I followed him up a wide staircase with a blood-red runner over marble steps and gilded balustrades. We paced through several enormous rooms with soaring ceilings, silk damask walls, and beautiful skylights that brightened the rooms even on a gray day like today.

The art and antiquities on display made my head

spin. Ornate French furniture, old Masters' paintings, Roman statuary, and Egyptian artifacts filled the rooms. My aunt and uncle lived in Parkview Hall, which had a nice stock of antiquities and beautiful paintings, but the contents of Mulvern House were astounding.

The butler entered a smaller room with a pale green silk damask on the walls along with several massive medieval tapestries. Crates were stacked around the room, and the aroma of straw filled the air. A woman was seated at a Louis XVI desk, which was covered with what looked like small brightly colored oval-shaped stones. A dark-haired man with a suntan who looked to be in his mid-thirties sat in a chair across from the desk. He wore an impeccably tailored double-breasted suit. I thought I saw a trace of annoyance in his close-set green eyes as his gaze flicked over me.

The butler announced me, and the man in the suit stood. "I didn't realize I was intruding on your social calendar, Lady Agnes," he said in a soft-spoken voice. "I'll leave you to your visitor, but do think on my offer. You'll not get anything better." He reached for a Homburg hat that rested on the corner of the desk. He didn't pause to be introduced, only nodded as he brushed by me. "You don't have to show me out, Boggs," he said to the butler. "I know the way."

Lady Agnes came toward me, her hand outstretched. "Miss Belgrave. Thank you for coming." She motioned to the door. "You'll have to excuse Mr. Dennett. He came to speak to me about Egyptian antiquities, and it's as if he has blinders when that subject is under discussion. He's just returned from Cairo and is in the grip of Egyptomania."

I hadn't met Lady Agnes. She spent most of her time in Egypt with her uncle on the excavations he sponsored, but I'd seen enough pictures of her in the society pages to recognize her. There was no mistaking her heart-shaped face and corkscrew raven curls, which were cut short in a bob that framed her large brown eyes. I thought perhaps she might be tanned from all her time spent in the Egyptian sun, but her complexion was a creamy porcelain except for a tinge of pink in her cheeks.

"It's my pleasure."

She wore a tunic-style dress in a black and red paisley print with a Mandarin collar. A wide cuff of glossy black fur edged the sleeves, and the dress floated with her movements as she turned to the butler. "Boggs, send up some refreshments."

"Yes, my lady," Boggs said and melted away.

A Siamese cat came out from under a desk, and Lady Agnes stooped to run her hand along its cream-colored fur as it curved by her legs. "This is Lapis."

"She's beautiful," I said, amazed at the cat's bright blue eyes.

"She certainly thinks so," Lady Agnes said with a grin.

Lapis gave my shoes a sniff, then sauntered over to the windowsill by the desk and leaped straight up into the air. She landed lightly on the ledge and spread out, tail trailing over the side.

Lady Agnes gestured to armchairs positioned in front of the fireplace, where a blaze crackled. "Please have a seat. It's turned so chilly I could do with a good hot cup of tea."

"Sounds lovely." I inched my way between the crates.

"Sorry about the crush." She waved a hand. "I'm finalizing items for the exhibit. Soon all this will be at the museum."

"The exhibit?"

"Uncle Lawrence was in the final stages of preparing for an exhibit of his Egyptian antiquities when he died." Her voice and manner up to that point had been forthright and matter-of-fact, but now sadness infused her tone.

"My condolences. I'm sorry for your loss."

"Thank you."

A maid entered with a tea tray and wove her way through the crates. Lady Agnes waited until the maid deposited the tea tray on a low table and left the room before she asked, "I suppose you've heard about the rumored curse?"

"I read about it in the newspapers."

Lady Agnes gave an irritated shake of her head as she poured. "I'm still amazed they're focusing on Uncle Lawrence."

I took the teacup from Lady Agnes. "Why is that?"

Lady Agnes's gaze went to the crates. "While Uncle Lawrence's finds are quite fascinating in themselves, they're nothing compared to the discovery of King Tutankhamen's tomb. The newspapers should concentrate on Mr. Carter and Lord Carnarvon's discoveries, not Uncle Lawrence's."

"I've found that newspapers rarely cover what one wishes they would."

Lady Agnes gave a small laugh. "So true, Miss

Belgrave. Unfortunately, I'm learning that. So what do you know about the situation surrounding my uncle?"

"Only what I've read in the newspapers. Perhaps you could tell me what happened, and then we can decide if I can be of help to you."

"Yes, of course." Lady Agnes sipped her tea. "Uncle Lawrence's valet couldn't rouse him one morning. It was September ninth."

So a little over a month before, which would account for the lack of mourning at Mulvern House and in Lady Agnes's clothing. The Great War had destroyed the strict rules about mourning attire and etiquette. I wasn't surprised to see no evidence of mourning in the town house, and Lady Agnes in bright colors. My Aunt Caroline would disapprove, but I didn't see anything wrong with limiting the external signs of mourning. I could see from Lady Agnes's somberness when she spoke of the death of her uncle that she was still mourning him.

"Uncle Lawrence left a brief note saying the horrors prevented him from going on. The press found out about the note. I have no idea how. The gossip sheets immediately latched onto the story. They reported Uncle Lawrence was driven to suicide by the curse." Lady Agnes's cup rattled as she put it down. "It's completely ridiculous. Besides the preposterous stories about the curse, the articles are inaccurate. They can't even spell the name of the mummy properly. They spelled it *Sozar*, which is completely wrong. It's Zozar, with a Z." She closed her eyes briefly and drew a breath. "Of course that's the *least* important thing."

Her agitation faded, and she fixed her dark gaze on me. "I want you to get to the bottom of this curse nonsense. My brother Gilbert is a bit of a rattle, but he does have a good heart. He doesn't deserve the treatment he's gotten from the press, which has painted him as an incompetent. It's true he doesn't have Uncle Lawrence's interest in Egyptology, but that doesn't mean Gilbert is a dunce. It's also upsetting my new sister-in-law, Nora." The mention of her sister-in-law seemed to be an afterthought.

Besides reading about the mummy curse in the newspaper, I was also aware of a rumor filtering through the high society set that Gilbert had been anxious to inherit his uncle's title and money. I knew Gilbert slightly, and in my encounters with him he'd seemed an affable, if slightly dense, young man. Should I mention the gossip? It was something I'd debated all morning, and I hadn't been able to decide on the best course of action.

If Lady Agnes took offense . . . well, my work with her would be over before it had begun. But Lady Agnes didn't seem to be the sort who ignored reality. No, I imagined she met challenges boldly. I cast around for the least offensive way to describe the rumors, but before I could speak, she said, "It's imperative the rumors are stopped—all of them."

Ah, so she was aware of the whispers about Gilbert. I took that to be a good sign. She didn't deny them out of hand or pretend they didn't exist—two options I'd found were never productive. "I understand your concern." I placed my empty teacup on the low table in front of me. "I do have one reservation." I wanted to help Lady Agnes and her family, but I didn't know if it would be possible. "It's difficult to disprove a suspicion. Even if I'm able to demonstrate the curse doesn't exist, that doesn't mean the papers won't continue writing stories about it."

"Oh, I don't want you to debunk the curse. I want you to prove Uncle Lawrence was murdered."

CHAPTER TWO

*B*efore I could respond to Lady Agnes's statement, the door burst open and a young woman strode into the room. Glossy golden-brown hair framed her delicate features, and she was dressed in an exquisite day dress of pale green. She would have been beautiful except for her sulky expression. I recognized her immediately. When I knew her at finishing school, Nora Clayton had long hair and had been a bit plumper, but she'd had the same confident manner. Her nickname at school was Narcissistic Nora—but it was only whispered about her, never said to her face.

A flash of movement out of the corner of my eye caught my attention. The Siamese cat, Lapis, jumped lightly to the floor in a silent sinewy movement.

"Agnes, you must hire a proper lady's maid for me," Nora said. "That creature who took Mary's place shattered my perfume bottle. Now my room positively reeks of lily of the valley."

Agnes gestured toward me. "We have a visitor,

Nora. Let me introduce you to Miss Olive Belgrave. She's here to help us with this silliness about the curse. Olive, this is my sister-in-law, Lady Mulvern."

"We were at finishing school together," I said. "Congratulations on your wedding." The wedding had taken place three months before. I hadn't been invited, but I hadn't expected to receive a gilt-edged invitation. Nora and I hadn't been close.

Nora flicked a glance my way. "Oh yes. I remember. You were the one who couldn't ski."

Lady Agnes's eyes widened at the casual rudeness, but I smoothed over the awkward moment. "My asthma does act up in cold, dry air."

"Lovely to see you again," Nora said without the least trace of sincerity, then switched her attention back to Agnes. "The stupid girl lost my gloves too. They're nowhere to be found. Dorothy will be here soon, and I must find them before I leave."

"You probably left them in a taxi, like you did with your handbag."

Nora's eyes narrowed. "I didn't leave my gloves in a taxi. It's easy to forget a handbag. One puts it down on the seat and then gets distracted, but I'd never take off my gloves in a taxi."

Lady Agnes ignored Nora's biting tone. "One would certainly hope not. Have a cup of tea before you leave." Lady Agnes didn't wait for a response but reached for the teapot. I knew I should think of Nora as Lady Mulvern, but it was hard to attach such a formal and imposing title to someone I'd seen clamber out a window to sneak a cigarette.

Lady Agnes poured the tea. "You can borrow a pair of my gloves. Speak to Carol about it."

I expected Nora to wave away the tea, but she came around the sofa and sat down. "No sugar or cream for me."

"Of course not." Lady Agnes handed the tea to Nora.

Nora looked at me over the rim of her cup as she sipped. "So you're the one who's going to do what the police wouldn't?"

"I'm sorry?" I'd always been wary of Nora. She reminded me of Lady Coddlingham's dachshund. During a dry spell when I had no other work, I'd searched for the dowager's lost dog. I'd found it huddled under a tree in the mews down the lane from the dowager's house. It had looked so darling with its limpid eyes and fluffy ears, but it had sunk its sharp teeth into my hand when I'd gone to pick it up.

"Agnes tried to convince the police that Uncle Lawrence was murdered, but she wasn't successful," Nora informed me, then turned to Lady Agnes. "Is it wise to pin your hopes on an amateur?"

Annoyance rippled through me at Nora's disdainful tone, but I tamped down my irritation. It wouldn't do any good to alienate her. Despite Nora's bad manners, she *was* Lady Mulvern. I ignored the barbs and focused on the information. "I didn't realize there was any question about the cause of Lord Mulvern's death," I said to Lady Agnes.

"Not for want of trying on Agnes's part," Nora said.

Lady Agnes cleared her throat. "Once the police saw the note on the desk in Uncle Lawrence's room, they didn't seek any more information, which is unacceptable."

After another tiny sip of tea, Nora put the cup down. "I don't see what the problem is. We all know who did it." Lapis, the Siamese cat, had made an unhurried circuit of the room and now paused at Nora's knee.

"You do?" My gaze skipped from Nora to Lady Agnes.

"It's perfectly obvious," Nora said. "Hodges did it."

"Hodges?" I asked.

Lady Agnes tilted her head slightly in acknowledgment of Nora's point. "It's possible. Lionel Hodges. Uncle Lawrence's valet."

"Uncle Lawrence left Hodges a bequest in his will." I'd expected Nora to ignore the cat or shoo it away, but she angled her knees slightly toward Lapis, and the cat sprang into her lap. "A very generous bequest." Nora ran her hand over the cat's head. She pitched her voice higher as she said, "Wasn't it, Lapis?"

Lapis closed her eyes and leaned into the stroking.

"Hodges had access to Uncle Lawrence's room, and he was the last person to see Uncle Lawrence alive." Nora lifted one shoulder. "As I said, it's obvious."

"So the household is convinced your uncle was murdered?" I asked.

Lady Agnes and Lady Mulvern exchanged a glance. I had a feeling the two women didn't see eye to eye on much, but this was one topic they were in agreement on. Lady Agnes said, "Some of us think that."

Nora added, "Of course my husband refuses to even consider Hodges might have had something to do with Uncle Lawrence's death." There was a strain in her voice that hadn't been there a moment before. The cat shook its head then jumped to the floor and padded to the window.

Nora looked at her wristwatch and popped up, brushing cat hair off her skirt. "I must fly. I'm sure Dorothy is here, and I can't miss my appointment with Madame LaFoy. I simply must have a new hat to go with my brown velvet. I have absolutely nothing that matches it."

She sailed out of the room without saying goodbye and pulled the door closed as she left. It slammed with a bang.

"Besides knowing how to make an entrance, Nora never skips a chance to make a dramatic exit," Lady Agnes said, then her expression turned more serious. "Perhaps we should talk about your fee?"

I shifted on the cushion. "To be perfectly honest, I don't know if I can help you."

Lady Agnes raised her eyebrows. "You don't seem anxious to work with me."

"Oh, I am. I'd love to delve into the situation and see if I can sort it out, but I don't want you to be disappointed."

"I'm rarely disappointed. I'm a realist. I know what I'm asking will be difficult but . . . well, we can't go on with the situation the way it is now. Let me tell you about my uncle. In fact . . ." She stood. "You should see his work. You'll have a better understanding then."

I thought she was going to take me over to the desk where the rocks were spread out or to one of the crates and let me look inside, but she strode to the door and opened it. "I think you need to see the grand gallery."

CHAPTER THREE

*W*e moved through a chain of rooms, each as opulent as the last. "Uncle Lawrence added the grand gallery after he inherited this house. Originally the house was U-shaped, with wings on the east and west sides extending from the front block. Uncle Lawrence added the grand gallery across the back of the house, connecting the east and west wings. He wanted a place to display the best of the antiquities he'd excavated. Here we are," she said as we came to set of double doors that were propped open.

So not quite the "locked up" situation the papers had described. I stepped into the room and the newspaper's description of supernatural mumbo-jumbo seemed utterly absurd. There was nothing frightening or eerie about the gallery.

It was decorated in the same style as the rest of the house, with sumptuous silk damask wall coverings, a coved ceiling with gilded accents, and an intricate parquet floor. Spectacular skylights ran the length of the narrow corridor of the room, which let in plenty of natural light, even on this overcast day. But I barely noticed the impressive setting. The antiquities dominated the grand gallery. Not two feet from me lay a stone sarcophagus—a term everyone knew because of the discovery of King Tutankhamen's tomb. Beyond it were several mummy coffins.

"Let me turn on the lights." Lady Agnes went to a panel on the wall. "We keep them off to preserve the colors."

She flicked a switch, and the vibrant colors of the coffins—ebony, lapis blue, and shimmering gold—glowed. A glass cabinet nearby contained fragile papyrus fragments, each with a translation card beside it. Another display case held ancient jewelry, row after row of intricately designed collars, cuffs, and earrings made with golden beads and precious stones. A line of coffins—at least ten or fifteen of them—stretched down the center of the room, each one in a glass display cabinet. Some of the coffin lids had been removed, revealing the yellowed linen wrappings of the mummies. "This is truly amazing," I said.

Lady Agnes smiled. "I agree. It's one of my favorite places. I often come here and wander around, admiring the artistry of the pieces."

I stepped closer to the nearest coffin. The vibrant colors, the intricate decoration, and the lifelike representation of a face with a delicate nose and dark outlines around the eyes were stunning. "This was one of three coffins made for a temple singer in Thebes." Lady Agnes motioned to the next two coffins in the row, which looked similar, but each was slightly smaller than the pervious one.

"Like Russian nesting dolls," I said.

"Exactly. Let me show you something else." Lady Agnes strolled down the gallery at a slow pace, which gave me time to examine the pieces. "My uncle was not a treasure hunter. Uncle Lawrence admired the gorgeous craftsmanship of the antiquities, but he was truly passionate about the scientific study of the Egyptian civilization."

We stopped in front of a plinth with a large oval pot. It had a wide rim and small handles. A boat with several oars decorated the reddish-brown pot. Lines scored the surface; tiny cracks, I thought. Then I realized the pot had been shattered into hundreds of pieces but then meticulously put back together. "Uncle Lawrence reassembled this pot. He thought every shard of pottery or scrap of fabric was just as important as the most magnificent treasure."

Lady Agnes opened a drawer in another cabinet and pulled out a sheaf of papers. "These are the field notes from the excavation in the winter of nineteen twenty."

Cramped writing covered the page, documenting the day's work. The notes were concise yet specific. I skimmed one page, which noted exactly where they dug, what the soil was like, the exact position of the objects they found, and the condition of those objects.

"Uncle Lawrence believed in going slowly and methodically." She tapped the papers. "A careful record like this will be invaluable to scholars in the future. We have photos, drawings, surveys, and summary reports of every excavation."

I handed the papers back. "I can see he wasn't a dabbler."

"Far from it." Lady Agnes put the papers away. "Of course Uncle Lawrence was excited when something gorgeous or beautiful or unusual was found, but his main goal was to progress through a dig rationally and dispassionately. He despised people who rushed in and cleared a tomb simply to get all the valuables out. He wanted everything done in an orderly way so we can understand as much as possible."

We resumed walking then paused beside the most ornate coffin in a glass case at the center of the room. A bird-like creature spread its wings from shoulder to shoulder. Rows of hieroglyphics in gold, green, red, and black covered the rest of the case. "This is Zozar, a temple administrator at Thebes."

"There's a mummy inside?"

"Oh yes. It was the last one Uncle Lawrence acquired, and he wanted it kept just as it is, with the coffin closed and Zozar inside."

As I admired the attention to detail in the decoration, Lady Agnes said, "My disposition is similar to Uncle Lawrence's. I like to look at things logically and carefully, but I'll be the first to admit I'm far from rational about his death."

Her voice caught on the last word. We were standing side by side, both of us facing the coffin. I didn't want to embarrass her by staring, but even in the fleeting glance, I could see her eyes were shiny.

I reached into my pocket for a handkerchief, but she drew in a deep breath and turned to face me, blinking quickly. "I'd like you to assess my uncle's death," she said, her voice firm. "You're an outsider. I realize you know Nora, but you're not a close friend. You're not a family member either. I'd like you to look at the situation and give . . . well, let's call it a second opinion."

"I want to help you, but I'm not logical—far from it, in fact." My friend Jasper was always telling me I rushed in headlong without thinking, but that was going too far, in my opinion. "I tend to be more . . . intuitive."

"But you've worked out what happened in some very—um—unpleasant situations."

"Yes, that's true."

"Then examine the situation, and tell me what you see. That's all I ask."

"I can do that."

"I believe you should come and stay here at Mulvern House with us for a few days. You can meet everyone and gather all the information."

"Thank you. I appreciate the offer, but it's not necessary. I'm in London—"

"Nonsense. You'll get on much better if you're here."

I decided not to argue. It was clear Lady Agnes had made up her mind, and I could tell that once she made a decision, she moved forward—a characteristic I understood completely.

"I'll add you to the guest list for the opening of the exhibit, which is on Thursday."

"I'd be delighted to attend."

"Excellent. Now—"

Brisk footsteps clicked on the parquet floor as a man in his early twenties with spectacles and unruly dark hair entered the room from the set of doors at the opposite end of the gallery. He glanced up from a paper, spotted Lady Agnes, and refocused his attention on the paper. As he walked, he ran his hand over his hair in an attempt to smooth it down, but the moment he stopped, bumps sprang up, creating deep contours in his hair.

"Lady Agnes, I must speak to you about the papyrus display." His words were rapid-fire. "Mr. Rathburn wants an extensive selection, but many of them are far too delicate to move. And then we've had another inquiry about unwrapping—" He looked up, noticed me, and frowned. A tall glass display cabinet had blocked me from his view until that moment. "—the mummy."

"I'll speak to Mr. Rathburn about the papyrus display," Lady Agnes said. "As to unwrapping Zozar or any of the other intact mummies, the answer is—as always—absolutely not. Now, let me introduce you. Miss Belgrave, this is Mr. Wilfred Nunn. Wilfred is our collection manager. Miss Belgrave is going to help us sort out this awful business about the curse and Uncle Lawrence's death."

"Pardon me. I didn't realize you had company, Lady Agnes." Nunn pushed his glasses up the bridge of his nose, then blinked several times as he focused on me. "Pleased to meet you, Miss Belgrave."

"Delighted to make your acquaintance, Mr. Nunn. What a fascinating job you have, managing the antiquities."

Nunn glanced around the room as if he'd forgotten it was packed full of Egyptian artifacts. "Yes, yes it is," he said, his attention already back on the paper he held.

"Are you sure about the mummy, Lady Agnes? It might be beneficial to unwrap it. It would distract the newspapers from their—ah—current topic. We could stage the event and invite scientists and scholars as well as a few hand-selected reporters. Give them something useful to cover, instead of . . ."

"No. It's out of the question. Uncle Lawrence wanted Zozar left exactly as he is. He believed it wouldn't be long before new techniques in addition to X-rays will allow us to study them without unwrapping them, and I agree."

"But consider the amulets inside the wrappings, the scarabs and jewelry. If we unwrap the mummies, we can study those items closely."

"No. They will be left exactly as they are."

Was there a flash of anger in Nunn's eyes? It was hard to tell. The light reflected off his glasses, hiding his gaze.

Lady Agnes turned to me. "Come, I'll take you to Uncle Lawrence's room. You can have a look around, and then perhaps send for your things. I hope you'll join us for dinner tonight."

"That would be lovely." What else could I say? Lady Agnes was a teeny bit like a steamroller.

CHAPTER FOUR

*L*ady Agnes switched off the lights in the grand gallery and took me up the next flight of stairs and along the wing on the west side of the house until we reached a room at the far end. She paused on the threshold. "We haven't made any changes to Uncle Lawrence's room. I can't quite bring myself to do so—at least until we know exactly what happened."

It was a spacious room in the front block of the town house with windows that looked out over the front of the house. Mist fogged the view of the trees in the park at the center of the square. Although the room contained a nice Queen Anne highboy, a bureau, and a four-poster bed with a canopy, the space felt Spartan. The only other pieces of furniture were a large grandfather clock and a writing desk. Two pots that looked similar to the one Lady Agnes had shown me in the grand gallery sat on the tallboy. They were the only decorative touches besides several framed photographs.

I followed Lady Agnes into the room and gave a little start of surprise as an Egyptian coffin came into view. It stood upright in a corner and wasn't nearly as ornate as the ones in the grand gallery. This one was painted wood and didn't have any inlays or embellishments besides the paint. The red had faded to a pinkish tone, and it was decorated sparingly with only a few rows of hieroglyphs. Instead of a sculpted face like I'd seen on some of the coffins in the grand gallery, the face was painted on a flat surface, but it still seemed as if the dark eyes with their thick black lines were staring across the room.

Lady Agnes said, "I should have warned you about that one. It does tend to surprise people. The housekeeper has to warn the new maids. I'm so used to it, I barely notice it."

Lady Agnes ran her hand over the shoulder of the case. "This was the first piece Uncle Lawrence collected. He was visiting a friend at their country estate. They'd been clearing out the attics and intended to toss it out." She motioned to the side where a rusted piece of metal had been attached. "They'd put a hinge on the lid and used it to store their hunting rifles—can you imagine? Uncle Lawrence only knew a smidgeon about Egyptology, but he knew this shouldn't be lost. It's not a first-class piece, but it was very dear to him."

Lady Agnes stepped away from the mummy and gestured to the doors on either side of the room. "It's a suite with dressing rooms on either end."

I was surprised that Nora hadn't already staked her claim on what was surely one of the nicest rooms in the town house. "I suppose Nora and your brother will want to move in here eventually."

"Nora wants nothing to do with this room," Lady Agnes said. "Despite all her modern ideas—she still insists on carrying a latchkey, even though she's married—she's superstitious."

Lady Agnes walked to one of the windows. "The views from this side of the house are the nicest, but Nora is easily spooked and doesn't want to sleep in a room where someone died. I haven't had the heart to tell her that Great Aunt Susan passed away in the bed she sleeps in now."

I gravitated toward the photos on the wall. One was of a woman with masses of dark hair and rather sad eyes.

Lady Agnes turned away from the window. "That was my Aunt Eleanor."

"I didn't realize your uncle had been married."

"Oh yes. She passed away last year. It was quite a blow to Uncle Lawrence, but he threw himself into the season in Egypt with renewed energy. I think it actually helped him get through the worst of it."

Obviously it was a sad subject and not one that Lady Agnes wanted to expand on, so I moved to the next photo of two children. A little girl of about five with curly dark hair stood clasping the hand of a taller boy with golden hair.

"This must be you." The dark hair and eyes were unmistakable, as was her pointed chin, which gave her a heart-shaped face.

"Yes, that was taken when Gilbert and I first came to live with Uncle Lawrence."

"You were quite young."

"Our parents were missionaries to Africa. They asked Uncle Lawrence and Aunt Eleanor to take care of us while they went out the first time to get settled. They intended to return within three months and take us back with them, but a fever swept through the village. They both died within days of each other. Uncle Lawrence and Aunt Eleanor were kind enough to adopt us."

"How tragic. I had no idea. I'm sorry."

"It was a long time ago," Lady Agnes said, her voice quiet. She stared at the photographs a moment, then turned away. "Of course that's why it's so important to me to find out what happened to Uncle Lawrence. Gilbert and I actually have very little family left. The thought that someone intentionally hurt Uncle Lawrence . . . well, I can't let it go until I know the truth."

"I'd feel exactly the same. Perhaps you could give me the details of what happened when your uncle died?"

"Of course." Lady Agnes's voice took on a brisk quality. She walked around the bed and motioned to a small table, which was bare except for a lamp. "At night Uncle Lawrence put his spectacles on this table, and Hodges always put out a tumbler along with a pitcher of water. It was a habit Uncle Lawrence had picked up in Egypt. It's so incredibly dry there, and he often had trouble with allergies. He took to keeping water on the bedside table. He continued to do so even here, despite it being so damp."

"And the police took away the water and the pitcher?"

"Yes. When Hodges found Uncle Lawrence in the morning, the glass was empty. The pitcher was about half full. Inspector Budge informed us that there was a residue in the tumbler, and it contained Veronal." Lady Agnes swallowed. "The concentration of it was quite high."

"And the pitcher of water?"

"It contained only water. The Veronal was found only in Uncle Lawrence's glass."

"Did your uncle take Veronal?"

"Occasionally. His allergies sometimes brought on the most awful aches in his head, and he'd take some Veronal before bed. The next day he'd be fine, but instances of him taking a sleeping draught were rare."

"So he had some Veronal in the room?" I asked.

She touched the drawer of the bedside table. "He kept a box of it here. We found six empty packets that morning."

I frowned. A box of the sleep aid contained small individually wrapped paper packets. Each tiny envelope contained several grains of the drug. I'd used Veronal before and dissolved one packet in a glass of water. Surely a man would only need two—maybe three—packets to induce sleep. If he'd opened several packets, Lord Lawrence *must* have known it would be dangerous, which was an argument completely counter to Lady Agnes's desire to prove her uncle didn't commit suicide. I wondered if anyone else in Mulvern House took Veronal. Of course it wasn't hard to obtain it from a chemist, so that was probably not a good line of inquiry.

Lady Agnes continued speaking, her gaze fixed on the bedside table. "Hodges prepared the room while we were at dinner. He said he filled the pitcher with water as he always did from the sink in the bathroom down the hall. He said he poured water into the tumbler, then left the pitcher beside it. Hodges swears he had nothing to do with any sleeping draught—that he'd never prepared one for Uncle Lawrence."

I had to admire her unflinching focus on setting down the facts for me. "I appreciate you telling me all this. I know it must be difficult."

Her shoulders sagged a few degrees. "It is painful." She straightened her posture. "But you must have all the facts to make an informed assessment. What else would you like to know?"

I glanced at the open door to the hallway. "Everyone in the house would have had access to the room?"

"That's right. The doors were open and unlocked. Anyone could have come in at some point that evening and added several packets of Veronal to his glass then slipped out again."

"Then let's make a list. Who was in the house that evening?"

"All the servants, of course, but they've all been with us for years and years. I can't imagine one of them suddenly poisoning my uncle."

"You've added no one new to the staff?" I asked.

"Only Boggs. He's been with us, let me think, over two months now. He came with excellent references, so he couldn't have had anything to do with it."

"And your previous butler?"

"Cleveland," she said with a smile. "He'd been our butler since I was a little girl. Uncle Lawrence provided a pension and a cottage for him on the estate in Devon. He's happily growing vegetable marrows now. I have no doubt he'll win prizes for them. Cleveland always does everything well."

"Who was at dinner that night?"

"It was a small party. I was Uncle Lawrence's hostess. Gilbert and Nora dined with us that evening. Wilfred Nunn and Albert Rathburn were with us as well."

I'd just met Wilfred Nunn, their collection manager, but I couldn't quite place the other name. "Albert Rathburn?"

"Keeper of Egyptian and Assyrian antiquities at the British Museum."

"Oh yes. His name sounded familiar. I believe I've read about him in the paper."

"One of the articles he's written, I imagine. He's been very vocal about lobbying the Egyptian government to send some of the treasures from Tutankhamen's tomb to the British Museum after it's opened. A losing battle, I think."

"Really? Why?"

"Because many Egyptians feel they've given away far too many of their treasures. I doubt much more will be approved for export in the future."

"Interesting. I had no idea."

"It's taken them years to establish a museum and develop an interest in preserving their own antiquities, but I think they've reached that point."

We'd gotten diverted, and as fascinating as the Egyptian antiquities were, I had to return to Lord Mulvern's death. "Did you notice if anyone was absent from the group that evening?"

A crease appeared between Lady Agnes's brows. "Not that I noticed. I suppose someone could have slipped out when we gathered in the drawing room either before or after dinner, but I don't remember. I wasn't keeping tabs on everyone."

"Of course not." I wasn't quite sure how to bring up my next question, but it had to be asked, so I plunged in. "I'm really very sorry to ask you this, but you mentioned there was a note?"

"Yes." Lady Agnes went to a desk positioned between the windows. She took out a piece of paper. "The police returned this after the verdict of death by misadventure."

She handed it to me. It contained a single sheet of paper. It was good stock, heavy and with a slightly rough texture. It was the sort of paper one expected to find in a house such as this.

The note was short and contained no salutation. It was not so much handwriting as scribbles. Each word began with distinct letters but then trailed off into a squiggle. I had to take a guess at the words, deciphering each from the legible letters at the beginning. "'I'm terribly sorry,'" I read aloud, deciphering the words. "'I cannot go on. The horror prevents me.'"

I looked up from the note. "This was all?" I flipped the page over, but the back was blank.

"Yes, that was all." Her voice sounded bleak, but there was a note of puzzlement in it as well.

"Something bothers you about this note."

She frowned at the note. "It just doesn't seem like the type of note Uncle Lawrence would leave if he intended to . . . do away with himself." She rubbed her temple and turned away for a moment, then swung back to me. "But that's the crux of the matter. I just don't believe Uncle Lawrence wanted to end his life."

"The tone of the note is certainly not what I'd expect either." While I'd never read a suicide note before, it didn't seem to be what one would leave for loved ones. It was so brief and didn't contain the emotion or the anguish I thought would be there.

"Which is one of the reasons I felt the whole thing is just a little—off," Lady Agnes said with renewed energy. "I knew my uncle very well. He was excited to catalog the most recent finds. And he was working on several scholarly papers as well as the museum exhibit. The other—and most important factor in my mind—is that he'd never been susceptible to any sort of superstitious nature. He laughed at the thought of curses. He didn't give the thought of a curse a moment's credence."

"It does sound as though he had a full schedule. Did he seem depressed or out-of-sorts?"

"Not at all," Lady Agnes said, her voice firm.

"I see." Had Lord Mulvern really been perfectly content with his life, or had he just hidden his distress well? I closed the folder and held it out to Lady Agnes.

She put up her hand. "Keep it." She must have seen the surprise in my expression because she added, "Please. I want you to have access to the note, this room, and everyone involved so you can conduct a thorough investigation. Just return it to me when you reach your conclusion."

"All right, I'll keep it if you insist." I said, but I felt uncomfortable about holding onto it. "Do you recognize the handwriting? It is your uncle's?"

"Oh yes," she said without hesitation. "I didn't have long to look at it when he was found, but there's no doubt in my mind that he wrote it."

"Perhaps we should talk about that. I presume he was found the next morning?"

Lady Agnes nodded. "Uncle Lawrence was always an early riser. Hodges brought his tea at six thirty and found him still in bed."

"Which was unusual?"

"Yes. I'm sure it happened occasionally, but Uncle Lawrence was one of those people who was up before sunrise and busy all day. When Hodges couldn't rouse him, he alerted the household."

"Who did he go to?"

"Me," said a masculine voice from the doorway.

Lady Agnes and I turned, and Lady Agnes held out a hand. "Gilbert, I didn't hear you there."

CHAPTER FIVE

*L*ady Agnes said, "Gilbert, come and meet Miss Belgrave."

Gilbert and his sister still had the contrasting looks so evident in the childhood photo. Where Lady Agnes had dark hair and eyes, Gilbert's hair was fair, and his eyes were a light blue. I'd met him briefly and remembered him as a rather rumpled young man with a casual, jolly manner. He crossed the room and took Lady Agnes's outstretched hand and patted it. "I thought I heard voices in here. Gave me quite a turn."

He shifted his attention to me. "No need to introduce us, Aggie. Delighted to see you again, Miss Belgrave. I believe we met at a picnic. The Daltons', wasn't it? I confess that afternoon is a bit fuzzy. Too many gin rickeys, don't you know."

"Yes, it was near the Thames. There was boating."

He still had that same mellow manner and easy smile.

"That's right. Thomas and Jigs managed to overturn the boat that we were in." He tilted his head toward Lady Agnes. "Which had nothing to do with the gin rickeys, I assure you."

"I find that highly doubtful," Lady Agnes said.

The dousing hadn't perturbed Gilbert. He'd brushed away the water and said, "Good thing it's a sunny day. It will dry." It seemed his lenient attitude about his appearance hadn't changed either. Today his coat didn't fit smoothly over his shoulders, his collar was crushed, and a trace of what looked to be jam spotted his tie.

Gilbert ignored the knowing look on Lady Agnes's face. "Are you enjoying the tour of Mulvern House, Miss Belgrave? Have you taken her to the grand gallery, Aggie?"

"We've just come from there," Lady Agnes said. "But I'm not showing her the house. Miss Belgrave is going to help me convince the police to reopen the investigation into Uncle Lawrence's death. She's agreed to take our case."

A frisson of excitement surged through me at her words—I had a case!—but I'd only agreed to give her my opinion after a thorough investigation of the facts. Before I could politely point that out, Gilbert cut his gaze in my direction. "Really?"

His tone suggested he expected Lady Agnes to declare her statement was a joke. But there was also another note I couldn't quite identify. Was it fear? I wasn't sure.

"Yes." Lady Agnes said, her voice adamant. "Miss Belgrave has recently had two successes in sorting out rather . . . um . . . delicate matters. I think she's the perfect person to help us."

"I see." A coolness infused his tone. The warm and affable man who had reminisced about summer boating had vanished. "I don't think it's a good idea to stir everything up again."

"Again?" Lady Agnes said. "Nothing's settled. Unless we do something, the newspapers will continue to bring up Uncle Lawrence's death again and again. I was just telling Miss Belgrave about that morning when Hodges found Uncle Lawrence."

"I don't think—"

"Yes, Gilbert, I know you don't think it's a good idea, but Miss Belgrave has already agreed. I'll go forward with you or without you, but I'd appreciate it if you'd tell Miss Belgrave what you remember about Uncle Lawrence's death."

Gilbert drew in a breath and let it out slowly. "All right, I'll give Miss Belgrave the details, but only because I know how you are, Aggie, when you get a bee in your bonnet." He looked at me out of the corner of his eye and some of his good humor returned to his attitude. "Completely unreasonable."

Lady Agnes raised an eyebrow but didn't bother to defend herself. "Go on, tell Miss Belgrave what happened."

"There's not much to tell, really." Gilbert sobered. He pulled at his wrinkled collar. "Hodges knocked on my door a little after six thirty. He told me the situation, and I came here with him." Gilbert halted, his gaze going to the four poster. "I could see from the first moment that Uncle Lawrence was gone. There was nothing to be done except send for the doctor, which we did immediately. Then I went to wake Aggie and Nora."

The order he named his relatives was interesting. I wondered if Gilbert really did find Aggie and tell her the news before he told his wife. And I hadn't missed another detail. Gilbert and Nora must have been sleeping in separate bedchambers if Nora hadn't been awakened when Hodges went to alert Gilbert. It wasn't that unusual for couples of their status to have separate bedchambers, but it seemed a little early in their marriage for them to be sleeping apart. But what did I know? I was an unmarried young woman.

Lady Agnes picked up the narrative. "It didn't take Dr. Thomas long to arrive. It was while he was here that I noticed the note on the desk." She ran her hand over a fur cuff of her dress as she spoke, stroking it in an absentminded way. "I went over and picked it up. That was when my hand began to shake—when I read it. My mind simply couldn't process the words on the page. Uncle Lawrence *wouldn't* commit suicide."

Gilbert put a hand on his sister's shoulder. "As the doctor told us, these things often don't make sense. You may have to accept that."

"No." She shrugged off his hand. "Not until we've explored every other option. The police did a slipshod job of looking into Uncle Lawrence's death. Once it's been thoroughly investigated, if there's no other answer . . . well, *then* I'll accept it. We have to know the truth. I won't accept supposition and conjecture."

Lady Agnes touched her forehead, and her fierce

tone faded. "I'm sorry, Gilbert. I shouldn't bite your head off like that. Forgive me."

"There's nothing to forgive. We're all a bit touchy. I'm sure Miss Belgrave understands and will make allowances for it."

"Of course," I said, trying to work out the dynamic between them. Lady Agnes had the more forceful personality of the siblings. Gilbert had yielded to her insistence I take on the case rather quickly, I thought. But apparently Lady Agnes did care what her brother thought of her and didn't want to hurt him.

"Did you want to ask Gilbert anything else?" Lady Agnes asked. "He has a tendency to disappear off to his club, so you should ask him now while he's here."

"Yes, a few things," I said, my mind spinning through possible questions. "Did anyone leave the drawing room the evening of the dinner party?"

"No, I don't think so," Gilbert said. "Rather hard to remember, you know. It was just a regular dinner party. We had no idea that the next morning . . ."

"Of course. But it could be important. Did anyone slip away?"

"No—well, when we left the table to join the ladies in the drawing room, Mr. Rathburn went to—um . . ."

"Use the facilities?" Lady Agnes asked, her distress at her outburst fading as she returned to her matter-of-fact manner.

Gilbert cleared his throat with a sidelong glance at her. "Um, yes, I believe so."

"Really, Gilbert, you don't have to be so namby-pamby," Lady Agnes said. "We're gathering facts here."

"That's correct," I said. "Anyone else?"

"No, not that I remember."

"And did you see anyone go into Lord Mulvern's room that evening?"

"Only Hodges, but that was perfectly normal."

"Did you go into his room?" I asked. I felt the weight of Lady Agnes's gaze on me as I waited for Gilbert to reply.

"Me? No—certainly not. I had no reason to."

"Calm down, Gilbert," Lady Agnes said. "Miss Belgrave isn't accusing you of anything, are you?" She emphasized the last two words, and I heard her warning.

"Certainly not. Simply gathering facts." I'd thought if Gilbert had stepped into his uncle's room, he might have noticed something unusual, but it seemed merely asking him if he'd entered the room bothered him, which was intriguing. I made a mental note to ask everyone if they'd actually stepped into Lord Mulvern's room so I could see their reaction.

Lady Agnes checked her wristwatch. "Well, I believe that's all we have time for now. Miss Belgrave is joining us for dinner tonight," she explained to Gilbert, then turned to me. "Mr. Rathburn is dining with us tonight as well. It will be a good opportunity for you to meet him and lay the groundwork for a future conversation about the dinner party that night."

"Good luck with that. Rathburn only talks about himself," Gilbert said.

Lady Agnes sent him a repressive look, but then said, "Mr. Rathburn can be a bit . . . challenging." Her tone changed as she said briskly, "Now, we still need to discuss your fee and send for your things, Miss

Belgrave." Gilbert looked puzzled, and Lady Agnes said to him, "Miss Belgrave is staying with us for a few days."

The news seemed to unsettle him, but then his good manners took over. "Happy to have you," he said before I followed Lady Agnes out of the room. I had the distinct impression he meant exactly the opposite.

CHAPTER SIX

*A*s I climbed the stairs to my attic room at Mrs. Gutler's boardinghouse, I couldn't help but notice the contrast between it and Mulvern House. The threadbare runner on the stairs barely dulled the sound of my footsteps, and the faded wallpaper peeled along the seams. But for all its shabbiness, the place was clean, and, under the gruff exterior Mrs. Gutler had initially projected, my landlady was kind and cheerful. Normally, she came out from the parlor or kitchen to greet me when I returned.

The kitchen door swung open. I looked over the railing, but it was Cook who emerged, drying her hands on a towel. "Mrs. Gutler's out—with that Mr. Sumpton." Cook added a sniff that conveyed her disapproval of the situation.

A war widow in straitened circumstances, Mrs. Gutler took in boarders to make ends meet, but lately, Mr. Sumpton, who lived around the corner, had become a frequent visitor. When I had asked Mrs. Gutler about him, she waved off any hint that romance was in the air, but blushed like a schoolgirl.

"Post's arrived," Cook said as she waved to the narrow table positioned on the landing of the stairs, then retreated to the kitchen.

I'd have liked a cup of tea, but the meager fee I paid to Mrs. Gutler only included my attic room and breakfast. While Mrs. Gutler had often sent tea up to my room when I arrived back after a long day of job hunting, Cook would never go out of her way for me.

I had a letter from Gwen, which I tore open as I climbed to the top floor.

Dear Olive,

Just a quick note because we're packing to leave and that's all I have time for. I'll write more once we're back at Parkview, I promise. The South of France was lovely. I find the sea enchanting and looked forward to a stroll along the boardwalk each day. Violet thought all the lounging about and watching the waves was incredibly tedious, but the trip has done wonders for her. Time away was exactly what she needed. She's as lively as ever—thank goodness.
We'll stop in Paris to visit the dressmakers, and I'll have some gorgeous frocks to show you when we return. I'll write as soon as we arrive at Parkview. You must come and stay for a good long visit. I feel it's been an age since we've been together.

Fondly,
Gwen

I refolded the letter and put it on the deal desk, which was wedged into the corner of my room. I'd write a reply before I left for Mulvern House with the news that I would be staying there in case Gwen returned soon. I doubted the stop in Paris would be brief. Aunt Caroline liked to be turned out in the latest fashions, and I was sure she'd take the opportunity to update Gwen and Violet's clothes as well.

I opened the doors to the wardrobe. Thanks to Gwen's generosity, I had plenty of nice day dresses and evening gowns. The hand-me-down evening gowns from Gwen were fabulous and something I could never afford. Gwen was several inches taller than me, so I had shortened the hems, which was all the adjustment the dresses needed.

I looked over the selection, considering the cool October weather. I'd visited a chum's during school holidays. The stately homes, while beautiful and grand, were also as cold as the family mausoleum. Mulvern House seem to be a well-run establishment and fairly modern. I didn't think I'd spend my time freezing and bundled in layers, but it never hurt to bring an extra shawl and cardigan. A trace of the chill and damp of October would be felt in even the most modern town house.

I took out several day dresses, then selected three evening dresses—a blue velvet with a beaded bodice, an emerald-green velvet with simple lines and no orna-mentation except a contrasting ruffle down the skirt in apple-green silk, and a teal silk. The silhouette of the teal dress with its fitted bodice and full skirt was falling out of fashion, but it would be warm and it was one of my favorite evening gowns because of the embroidered peach-colored flowers on the bodice and skirt. Lady Agnes would expect me to return with a maid, but my funds didn't run to employing someone. I was just beginning to feel as if I was on a more secure financial footing, but I certainly couldn't pay someone's wages at this point. I cared for all my own clothes. I sent them out to be washed at the little laundry nearby, and I was the one who repaired seams or switched out bits of braid or feathers to refurbish my hats.

I was packing my clothes when a tap on the door sounded. Mrs. Gutler, still in her hat and gloves, held out a small brown paper bundle. "Just arrived for you, dearie."

"Thank you, Mrs. Gutler."

She looked over my shoulder to my clothes spread across the bed and my open suitcase. "Oh, off to another grand house, are you?"

"I've been invited to stay at Mulvern House."

Mrs. Gutler's hand went to her throat. "You're not going, are you? Not with that horrible curse?"

"There is no curse. You know those articles in the newspaper are exaggerations. I told you they completely distorted what happened at Archly Manner and at Blackburn Hall. Everything will be fine at Mulvern House."

"Well, I don't like it."

"It's only for a few days," I said. "You'll forward any letters I receive, won't you?"

"Of course. But I don't like it. That mummy looked

quite ferocious. There was an illustration of it in the paper yesterday, you know."

"I went there this morning and everything was perfectly normal."

Mrs. Gutler shook her head. "You young girls are so brave . . ." She tilted her head. "Or foolhardy. I can't quite decide which it is."

I assured her again that I'd be fine. After she left, I examined the address on the package.

It was from Jasper Rimington, a good friend. I still felt a flare of irritation at the way he'd disappeared from Blackburn Hall, but I was glad to have some sort of communication from him. I moved the dresses, and the bed springs squeaked as I settled down to open the package.

I ripped it open and sucked in a breath. A gun lay nestled in the torn paper, but there was something about it—something not quite right. I picked it up. The handle fit into the palm of my hand, but it didn't have the weight I expected, and there was a tiny hinge on the top. I turned it over and found a little clasp under the trigger.

I flicked the clasp, and the "gun" opened, revealing a mirror, a powder puff, and a tiny indentation for a latchkey—it was a makeup compact. I'd seen compacts in plenty of different shapes and designs but never one that looked like this. I snapped it closed and turned it over again in my hand. It was cleverly made. Someone would have to look closely to see it wasn't a real gun.

A cream-colored envelope rested in the packaging. I recognized Jasper's neat handwriting. He'd printed my name in his exact strokes.

Olive, old girl, I hope you will accept this rather interesting gift. I saw it in a window and thought it would be perfect for you. You've gotten into a few sticky situations, and having something that appears to be a weapon could be to your advantage. Hope you are well and never in a position where you need your "gun" compact.

Very sincerely yours,
Jasper

I couldn't help but smile and think how scandalized Mrs. Gutler would be if she were to catch a glimpse of the compact.

I sat down and wrote to Gwen with the news I'd been invited to Mulvern House.

Next, I wrote to my boarding-school chum Essie, who now worked at *The Hullabaloo,* and asked if she could meet me the next day. I'd have to be careful what I told her because Essie tended to convert even passing comments into news for her society column, but if there was anyone who could find out who was leaking information to the newspapers, it was Essie.

Then I penned Jasper a quick note of thanks before I tucked the compact into my small handbag. It fit easily. I finished packing and set out for Mulvern House.

CHAPTER SEVEN

hen I returned to Mulvern House, Lady Agnes met me at the door and took my lack of maid in stride. "You can borrow Martha," she said as she guided me upstairs to the wing on the west side of the house, where the family had their rooms. She opened the door on a spacious room with Sheraton furniture. The walls were covered with a pale blue silk damask that matched the bed covering and upholstered chairs in front of the window. Bowls of gold carnations were dotted about the room. "What a lovely room."

"It's one of my favorites." Lady Agnes glanced at her wristwatch. "I'm afraid you won't have much time to change for dinner. I'll send Martha straightaway. We'll meet in the drawing room in half an hour."

I was quite used to doing for myself, so half an hour wasn't a problem. Martha was a young girl of about seventeen with a frizz of fair hair poking out from under her cap. By the time she arrived, I'd already changed into the teal silk evening dress with the fitted

49

bodice. All Martha had to do was help me with my hair, which didn't take long because it was bobbed, and then hand me my gloves.

When I joined the family in the dining room, Lady Agnes was speaking to the butler, Nora was seated in front of the fire, and Gilbert was sorting out bottles and glasses at the drinks cart. A rotund man in his sixties with a head of white hair and a white beard that covered his collar had cornered Wilfred Nunn and was delivering what seemed to be a speech about a trip down the Nile.

Gilbert picked up the cocktail shaker. "I believe I'll have a raspberry fizz. Nora?" he asked, a challenge in his words.

"I'll pass," Nora said.

"Olive?" Gilbert asked over the clatter of ice.

"A small one." I needed to keep a clear head this evening. I sat down by Nora. "I hope we'll have a chance to talk either tonight or tomorrow about the dinner party Lord Mulvern hosted before he died. I have a few questions about it."

"You're not going to be like that horrid policeman and ask endless questions, are you? I already told you—Hodges did it."

"I intend to talk to him, but he wasn't at the dinner. You were and might have noticed something important."

"I doubt it. I'm not the observant sort like you," she said, her tone indicating she didn't mean it as a compliment. "But since Aggie's made it clear we have to cooperate with you, go ahead, ask me whatever you must."

She might as well have added, *so I can get this over*

with. I ignored her bad manners and asked, "Did you notice anyone absent from the drawing room either before or after the dinner?"

Nora had been brushing a cream-colored cat hair off her arm, but she looked sharply at me. "Why?"

"I just need to know where everyone was."

Gilbert rattled the cocktail shaker, and she paused because it was too loud to speak over it. By the time he'd stopped, she'd regained her attitude of bored dissatisfaction. "I couldn't say. It was one of those stultifying evenings. Unbelievably tedious, more so than usual because we'd gone to the opening of the Bluebird the evening before with Mr. Dennett and Dorothy and I had an absolutely smashing time, which made the next night seem unbearably flat."

"Mr. Rathburn was here, correct?" I asked as Gilbert brought me a narrow glass with fresh raspberries floating in the drink.

"Yes, so tiresome. You'll see. After dinner you'll understand exactly what I mean."

"Did you see anyone go in Lord Mulvern's room that evening?"

"No."

"Did you go into his room anytime that evening?" I asked.

"Of course not. I—"

Gilbert returned with two more highball glasses garnished with raspberries. He sat down in a chair by Nora and put down one of the glasses on the table at Nora's side.

She drew back her arm as if she'd been stung by a bee. "Gilbert, I said I didn't want one."

"In case you change your mind," Gilbert said. "It's your favorite."

"It used to be."

They stared at each other a moment, tension in the air between them. I was glad to see Lady Agnes approach before their spat escalated. It didn't seem I would get any more details out of Nora about the dinner party since Nora clearly thought I should concentrate on Hodges. I went with Lady Agnes to meet the white-haired dinner guest, who still had Nunn buttonholed.

Lady Agnes broke into the older man's monologue and introduced me to him. "Albert Rathburn, the Keeper of Egyptian and Syrian Antiquities at the British Museum. Olive is our guest for a few days. She's recently moved to London from Derbyshire."

So Lady Agnes had done her homework on me. She hadn't asked me about my background earlier that day.

"Pleasure," Rathburn said. "I was just telling this young whippersnapper here about my time in Cairo." He lifted his cocktail at Nunn, who pushed his glasses up his nose and inched away, but Rathburn caught his arm. "Rather an eventful journey, if I do say so myself. It was on that trip that I tracked down the museum's most famous papyrus, and that's quite a story, let me tell you."

Still holding onto Nunn's arm and giving it a shake occasionally to emphasize a point, Rathburn launched into a story involving antiquities dealers, Egyptian government officials, and a gaggle of tourists. Apparently, the man was such a bore he had to physically restrain his listeners or they tried to escape, never a good sign in a dinner guest. With his round shape and downy white hair and beard, his appearance reminded me of Father Christmas. But instead of a cheerful demeanor, he seemed to have a single-minded determination to convey as much information about himself as possible.

My gaze wandered around the room during Rathburn's story. He didn't expect any responses from his audience, so I was able to note Nora and Gilbert sat in silence, their postures stiff. Gilbert finished his drink, then sipped from the untouched drink he'd brought to Nora.

Rathburn's tale lasted until dinner was announced. As we filtered out of the drawing room, I noticed Nora hung back a moment, then took a large gulp of what remained of her raspberry fizz when Gilbert's back was turned. Was she making a point by not drinking the raspberry fizz, or was it simpler? She hadn't taken cream or sugar in her tea earlier. Maybe she was watching what she ate—and drank—so she'd fit into her designer dresses.

I was seated by Rathburn at dinner, and he continued the papyrus story, droning on, communicating in paragraphs rather than sentences. I attempted to subtly work in the topic of the dinner party Rathburn attended before Lord Mulvern's death. I was curious about his perspective on the evening, but he batted the questions away and immediately returned to his favorite subject, himself. I gave up trying to wrest the conversation in a different direction after several failed attempts. Rathburn continued to rumble while I watched Gilbert and Nora, who were seated at the head and foot of the long table. They avoided eye contact, and Nora only ate a few bites of each dish.

". . . so do you know what I did?" Rathburn asked.

I gave a little start. Thank goodness I'd been listening with one ear. "I can't imagine one would have many options when one is locked in an Egyptian prison."

"That's where you're wrong. These Egyptian fellows are quite susceptible to bribery. Fortunately, I'd hired a guide who knew this, and he orchestrated an exchange of funds for my release."

"Indeed?"

"I've found it's the only way to do business in Egypt."

Across the table from me, Nunn sat immobile, his pudding untouched as he clenched his cutlery. I was rather glad his angry gaze was directed at Rathburn and not me. When I'd met Nunn that afternoon, I'd thought he had a rather mild, subdued personality, but he obviously had a depth of feeling and was struggling to maintain his composure. His voice tight, he said, "I believe that is a gross exaggeration."

Rathburn took a swig of wine. "How many times have you been to Egypt? Once? Twice? I've traveled there dozens of times. You've not been there enough to understand how things work." The footman placed a dessert plate in front of Rathburn. "Oh, apple charlotte, my favorite." He shifted in his chair and looked toward Lady Agnes. "I always enjoy dining with your family, Lady Agnes. Kind of you to remember my favorite."

Lady Agnes, who was not seated at the head of the table, smiled politely and tilted her head in Nora's direction. "I'm delighted to hear it, Mr. Rathburn. But it was Nora who arranged the menus for this evening."

Nora had been pushing the pudding around on her plate. "I did?"

"In your meetings with the cook and housekeeper," Lady Agnes said. "You went over the menus for the week."

"Oh, that. Yes, I suppose so."

But Rathburn was not to be distracted from himself too long. He consumed his pudding quickly, then launched back into his story, directing most of his comments to me. "You haven't heard the best part of the Luxor story. Once I was out of the jail, I was still determined to get the papyrus. It was exquisite—like nothing I'd ever seen. My guide had learned the papyrus had been taken from the dealer who'd been holding it for me. The Egyptian officials had transferred it to a house in Luxor and had the place under guard. So I scouted it out and found it was conveniently located next to the Luxor Hotel's garden. I immediately took a room and demanded to see the manager. After only a few moments, I convinced him to help me." Rathburn flicked his gaze across the table to Nunn for just a moment. "The liberal application of funds did not hurt there either."

Nunn's hand tightened on the stem of his wine glass, but before he could speak, Rathburn went on, "I sent my guide out to hire several sturdy men. I set the men to the garden to work. I gave them orders to do everything in complete silence because there were guards patrolling around the adjoining house. The men tunneled under the garden wall and into the basement of the house, where the papyrus was kept. I was quite impressed with their workmanship. They shored up the tunnel and made sure it wouldn't collapse." Rathburn grinned and might have been an illustration on a Christmas card, except for the jarring note of his glee at the underhanded tactics.

"I had a distinct feeling the men had done this before—quite often. Probably cleaned out the tombs of their ancestors many times." Rathburn chuckled and reached for his wine. "It was but a moment's work for them. They handed the papyrus to me before sunrise. By the time the Egyptian officials realized what had happened, I was on my way back to Cairo." He shrugged. "All I had to do was see the papyrus was in the diplomatic packet, and it was as good as home." He raised his glass. "And all Egypt rejoiced. I'd saved the Papyrus of Amun-su."

After an awkward moment, Gilbert lifted his glass a few inches in acknowledgment and took a sip. "A rousing yarn, indeed. But it doesn't seem quite cricket. Stealing it out from under them, especially when they decided they didn't want you to have it."

Rathburn waved a pudgy hand. "Not the case at all. The antiquities director in Egypt wasn't saving it for his country. He merely wanted to auction it off to the highest bidder. What better place for the papyrus to go than the British Museum, where it is carefully preserved and available to be studied? If I hadn't taken it, who knows where it could have ended up—or quite possibly even been destroyed.

"That silly chap Petrie sent several mummies from the Roman period to the Egyptian antiquities officials for their newly constructed museum—and they left them outside! They were only concerned with the oil paintings on the wood, which were attached to the mummies, *those* they brought in. No, there's a shocking lack of appreciation in Egypt for their own history."

Nunn's face had gone white. "I believe what you've done is wrong. There is no excuse for it," he said, his words clipped.

Lady Agnes cleared her throat and gave Nora a significant look.

"Oh—right." Nora pushed back her chair. "Ladies, let's leave the gentlemen to their port."

Gilbert must have sensed that things wouldn't go well with only himself, Rathburn, and Nunn because the men joined us in the drawing room soon after. Rathburn announced he had an early meeting and had to leave as he bowed over Lady Agnes's hand. "But I will be in touch with you soon about the exhibit's final details."

"Yes, we have much to discuss."

Once Rathburn departed, it seemed everyone in the room took a collective breath of relief. Nora immediately announced she was exhausted and went upstairs without a single look in Gilbert's direction. His gaze tracked her as she crossed to the door, but he didn't have the look of love on his face that I'd expect from a man married only a few months.

The evening ended soon after that, with the rest of us departing for our rooms. Lady Agnes walked upstairs with me. "I caught Mr. Rathburn before he left and told him you'd want to talk with him. If you go to his office at the British Museum tomorrow afternoon, he'll see you."

"Thank you, that's helpful."

"Good night, Miss Belgrave. I look forward to hearing what you discover."

I wished her a good night, and I went into my room with my thoughts chasing as Martha helped me out of my evening gown. Was the tension between Gilbert and Nora normal? And was there a hint of extra meaning layered in Lady Agnes's tone when she agreed with Rathburn that they had much to discuss?

I dismissed Martha and took a seat at the writing desk. I wasn't the least bit tired, and I wanted to look more closely at Lord Mulvern's suicide note.

CHAPTER EIGHT

'd placed Lord Mulvern's note in the drawer of the writing desk in my room that afternoon. I took it out and clicked on the desk lamp. Under the warm glow of the light, the brevity of the note gave it a feeling of curtness. It wasn't much of a note to leave —hardly any explanation—but if he wasn't quite in his right mind, that might explain the short length.

I studied the missive awhile, considering the individual strokes, but Lady Agnes had assured me it was her uncle's handwriting. I could see why Lord Mulvern had employed a secretary. His penmanship was indeed atrocious. The letters were smashed together to the point that only the first letters of the words were distinct. The letters in the middle were mushed blots of ink.

After a few more minutes of staring at it without any great discovery, I opened the drawer for an envelope. Lady Agnes had entrusted this letter to me, and I felt I should do everything I could to protect it.

But there were no envelopes in the center drawer. I quickly opened and closed the rest of the drawers. The desk contained writing paper—one stack of paper engraved with the words *Mulvern House* and the address, and another stack of plain pages—but no envelopes. The maid must have forgotten to restock them. I could ring and ask for envelopes, but it was late and could wait until later. I took out a blank sheet of writing paper and folded Lord Mulvern's note within the new piece of paper to protect it.

I immediately unfolded the two sheets and compared them. The suicide note was slightly smaller than the writing paper I'd taken from the desk. The edges on the left and right aligned with the page I'd taken from the drawer, but when I'd tapped the two pages on the desk, the top edge of the suicide note was shorter.

I held up both pages to the light. They each had the same watermark. They were the same shade of white, and they each had the same slightly rough texture of quality paper stock. If Lord Mulvern had written this note on paper taken from the desk in his room, why was the suicide note smaller?

I fanned through the two stacks of paper provided in the center drawer. They were all the same size. I picked up the suicide note and held it up to the light, then I aligned it with a fresh sheet of writing paper. The top edge of the suicide note wasn't square. It sloped slightly from the right-hand side of the page down to the left-hand side.

The change was so tiny, it was barely discernible. I held the suicide note up to the lampshade and traced my finger over the top edge. Two tiny bumps, slight notches, brushed against my fingertips.

I frowned at the paper for a moment. Before I made any assumptions, I had to see if the same writing paper was in Lord Mulvern's room. I refolded the suicide note within the larger sheet of paper, then put it in the pocket of my dressing gown. My room was near the stairs. Lord Mulvern's room was at the opposite end of the passageway, which was empty.

I padded along, glad the carpeted runner down the hallway deadened my steps. The door to Lord Mulvern's room stood open. A lamp positioned on a table in the passage threw an oblong of light into the room, which gave me enough illumination to distinguish the lamp on the bedside table. I switched on the lamp, then went back and closed the door to the hall. I felt as if I were trespassing, and it seemed that the eyes of the mummy case tracked me as I moved back and forth across the room.

I shook off the superstitious feeling and went to Lord Mulvern's desk, which was much larger than the one in my room. A burgundy leather inlay covered the top, and a multitude of scratches showed the desk was well used.

The middle drawer contained two stacks of writing paper as my desk did—one engraved, one plain. I fingered a sheet of the plain paper. It was the same weight and color as the suicide note. I held it and compared it to the suicide note, turning so I could compare the size of the sheets against the light from the lamp. The suicide note was again shorter.

The desk only contained two other drawers. The one

on the left was empty, and the one on the right held a couple of pens, a pair of scissors, and a few paperclips and rubber bands.

After a bit of debate, I picked up the scissors. Obviously, the desk had been cleared out and any personal belongings of Lord Mulvern's had been collected and removed. I was sure someone else—probably a maid—had handled these scissors between the time Lord Mulvern had died and now.

I snipped off the top edge of the plain sheet of writing paper I'd taken from Lord Mulvern's desk. I was careful to keep the scissors level and make the cut as straight as possible. The strip of paper fell away, and I held up my handiwork, comparing it to Lord Mulvern's note. Little notches along the top edge corresponded to the places where I had to open the scissors and reposition them to cut further along the paper. The notches were at roughly one-third and two-thirds of the way across the top of the page, which were the same spots as the notches on the suicide note.

I added the new blank sheet of paper that I'd just trimmed to my stack with Lord Mulvern's note. Then I took an envelope from the center drawer and slipped my packet of papers inside it. I closed the drawers and glanced over my shoulder. The dark-eyed gaze of the mummy coffin stared across the room, which was still a bit unnerving.

I clicked off the lamp and felt my way to the door, telling myself not to be a rabbit. The mummy coffin was a beautifully crafted relic from antiquity. There was nothing spooky about it.

But I couldn't keep myself from scurrying through

the darkness. I let out a breath once I was in the empty corridor. On my way back to my room, I tried to work out what I'd discovered.

It might have meant nothing. Perhaps Lord Mulvern was thrifty and had simply reused an old sheet of paper that the top edge had been trimmed off for some reason. But it could also mean that someone had tampered with Lord Mulvern's note. Perhaps it wasn't a suicide note at all—until someone had gotten a hold of it and snipped off the top portion. Of course, it would be impossible to prove that had happened. I was sure that if someone had modified Lord Mulvern's note, they wouldn't be stupid and discard the top strip of paper in a place like the wastepaper bin in his room.

I was sure the bit of paper that had been removed— if it was important—was either in ashes or had been disposed of in a way that it wouldn't be found. I closed the door to my room and let out a long breath, glad I hadn't met anyone in the passageway. Should I take my discovery to Lady Agnes?

No, not right away, I decided. I needed to gather more details about what had happened the night Lord Mulvern died. The fact that the note had been trimmed wasn't conclusive . . . but it was suggestive. Perhaps Lady Agnes was right and it wasn't her uncle who'd poured too much Veronal into his tumbler that night.

CHAPTER NINE

$\mathcal{I}$ came awake suddenly, my heart thudding. The shapes of the furniture in the shadowy room were all wrong, and the room itself was far too spacious. Then I remembered—I was at Mulvern House. The pale gray light of dawn filtered into the room through a gap in the drapes, but the room was still dark. I switched on the light on the bedside table. The clock showed it was a little after six in the morning.

A burst of sound, a piercing scream, pulsed through the air—*that* was the sound that had woken me. I tossed back the sheets and picked up my dressing gown. When I opened my door, a couple of doors down the hallway were open. Lady Agnes was already halfway down the stairs, the silky panels of her cream-colored kimono flaring around her legs as she hurried in the direction of the continuing screams, which were coming from the floor below.

A door jerked open, and Nora poked her head out, her gauzy dressing gown swirling around her. "What is that horrible racket?" Her hair was pressed flat to her head in pin curls. The criss-crossed bobby pins glinted in the light left burning on a table in the hall, making it look as if she were wearing some sort of metal helmet.

Gilbert emerged from the door next to Nora's, tying his brocaded dressing gown. "Rather a frightful cater-wauling, isn't it?"

"Put a stop to it." Nora slammed her door.

I raised my eyebrows. Someone definitely wasn't a morning person. I trotted down the stairs with Gilbert trailing behind me.

The high-pitched screams broke off. I rounded the corner and caught up with Lady Agnes at the doorway to the grand gallery. The hall was dim, but the lights were on. Agnes had an arm around the shoulders of a young maid, who was fighting back tears. A bucket lay on its side near the girl's feet, and a puddle of soapy water was spreading around a discarded mop across the parquet. "I'm so sorry, milady," the maid said between sniffs. "But it was the mummy. The mummy is out of its case."

I picked up the mop and propped it against the wall.

"Nonsense," Lady Agnes said. "I'm sure it's just your imagination."

"No, it's not," the maid said, then blinked and ducked her head. "I'm sorry, milady, but it's not in the case—it's *not*."

Boggs appeared, climbing the stairs from the main floor. He was in shirtsleeves, and the part in his gray hair was off-center. Another maid came up the stairs behind him, angling her head as she tried to see around Boggs into the grand gallery.

Lady Agnes propelled the sniffling maid in the direction of the second maid. "Louise had a bit of a fright. Take her downstairs and see she has a cup of tea with plenty of sugar in it." As the maids departed and Boggs informed Lady Agnes he'd have the mess cleared up, I stepped around the soapy water and into the grand gallery. It seemed glaringly bright after the shadows of the hall.

I'd expected to find the room exactly as it had been the day before, but I stopped short. "Good heavens. She's right."

One of the glass cases enclosing the mummy coffins at the center of the room was open. It had a hinge, and the top had been folded back. The lid of the coffin had been moved, and it rested in the aisle on the parquet. A few bits of linen were scattered on the floor like confetti leftover from a party.

Lady Agnes halted beside me. "The mummy *has* been disturbed." Her tone contained amazement and also a grimness that had me turning to look at her. "It's the mummy of Zozar," she explained. "The one that hadn't been unwrapped."

Lady Agnes strode quickly down the gallery, then stopped by the open glass case, hands on her hips as she surveyed the damage. I approached slowly. I considered myself an adventurous sort, but I wasn't at all sure I wanted to see an unwrapped mummy. But when I inched closer, I realized the linen hadn't been completely removed. A few strips of cloth had been peeled back, and a couple of fragments littered the floor, but the main damage to the wrappings were several deep cuts.

The blue embroidered dragon on the back of Lady Agnes's kimono shifted as she breathed heavily. "This is outrageous! I can't believe—"

Gilbert moved around to stand on the other side of the glass case, his arms crossed as his gaze skimmed over the rips in the linen. "What a mess. Well, it looks like we won't be able to keep this mummy under wraps any longer." A smile flickered at the corners of his mouth.

Lady Agnes sent him a look. "This is no joking matter."

"Sorry, sis. I know that, but I couldn't resist." Gilbert shook his head as his gaze traveled up and down the mummy. "Looks like they hit the old boy pretty hard. Do you think everything's gone?"

"I have no doubt that anything of value has been removed."

"Removed?" I asked.

"See these cuts here?" Lady Agnes said. "Mummies were buried with amulets and jewelry wrapped into the layers of linen. Whoever did this knew exactly where to find the heart scarab and jewelry." She touched a piece of cloth that had been pulled away. "This was just for show."

Footsteps pounded across the floor as Nunn sprinted the length of the room then jerked to a stop beside me. His flannel dressing gown hung open over a pair of faded pajamas. His glasses were askew, and some sections of his hair puffed up in unruly tufts while the rest was smashed flat to his crown. "Zozar." He spoke the mummy's name as if it were a friend, and his expression behind his crooked spectacles was one of almost mourning. He turned sharply to Lady Agnes. "This wouldn't have happened if you'd allowed us to unwrap the mummy."

"Perhaps," Lady Agnes said, her tone frosty.

Nunn swallowed and straightened his glasses. "I'm sorry—I spoke too hastily." He took a step back.

Lady Agnes sighed. "You may be right. But there's nothing we can do about it now except contact the police."

"The police?" Nora asked. Her curiosity must have gotten the better of her, and she'd come down the stairs after Gilbert. Without her makeup she looked much younger and rather plain. She hovered several feet away from the mummy. "Surely there's no need to do that."

"We must. There's been a theft." Lady Agnes looked at Gilbert.

He sent Nora an apologetic glance. "Aggie is right, old bean. I'm afraid we'll have to endure Inspector Thorn."

"Oh, I do hope they send someone else," Nora said. "He's one of those people who's never in a good mood, and being awoken at this time of the morning will only make it worse."

Nora was exactly right about Inspector Thorn's attitude. He was a compact, lean man, barely taller than me, and seemed to have a perpetual scowl fixed on his wrinkled face. He was clearly a chain smoker because Lady Agnes sent for a maid to bring an ashtray to the grand gallery for him. In between puffs on his cigarette, Thorn said, "You summoned me at this ungodly hour to look at a *mummy?*"

Lady Agnes ignored Thorn's statement and summarized the situation for him. "Nothing has been touched," she said. "I suppose you'll want to get your fingerprint men on it straightaway."

Inspector Thorn removed the cigarette from his mouth, and I took a step back. The acrid smoke from cigarettes seemed to trigger my asthma. "Won't do any good. Criminals know all too well the importance of wearing gloves." Inspector Thorn squatted and peered up at the open glass lid, his head tilted at an angle. "No, I don't see any smudges. I doubt we'll find anything."

"But you will search for fingerprints, won't you?" Lady Agnes's tone indicated there was only one correct answer to her question.

He stood, drew on his cigarette, and blew out a long stream of smoke as he looked from the mummy back to Lady Agnes. "Because it's important to you, I'll call the boys in. But don't get your hopes up." He turned to leave. "I'll be in touch if anything is found."

"Surely you're not leaving?" Lady Agnes asked, halting him before he'd gone more than two steps. "You need to interview everyone and confirm each person's whereabouts during the night."

"Lady Agnes, with all due respect, I realize that these mummies are important to you. But compared to the three murders, assault, and possible arson case, this"—he jabbed his cigarette at the mummy—"pales in comparison."

"Valuable objects that could contribute to our

knowledge of an ancient civilization have been lost." Lady Agnes's hands fisted at her sides. "Are you saying that nothing will be done?"

"No. It will be investigated. But we don't have much to work with here." He waved his hand back and forth over the Zozar mummy, trailing cigarette smoke. The ash on the end of his cigarette trembled, and Lady Agnes tensed. Thorn went on, "You said yourself that you can't describe the stolen gewgaws."

Gilbert stepped forward. "I say, bit dangerous waving that gasper over a mummy. Centuries-old linen, you know. Be a good fellow and step back."

I was surprised Gilbert intervened. He might not share his sister's passion for Egyptology, but he had some concern about the antiquities.

Inspector Thorn's scowl deepened, but he did move back as he continued speaking to Lady Agnes. "We'll do all we can, but you have no descriptions for me to circulate to the pawnbrokers. For all we know, it might be an inside job." He glanced from face to face. "You might not like the direction this investigation goes. Certain parties might find it . . . uncomfortable." His gaze lingered on Nunn, who shifted his feet and looked away. The inspector transferred his glare to me. "Who's this? A new addition from the last time I was called in, I think."

"This is my friend, Olive Belgrave," Lady Agnes said. "Miss Belgrave is staying with us for a few days. She had nothing to do with any of this."

With everyone else, Lady Agnes had been quite straightforward about why I was staying at Mulvern House, but she must have realized that announcing I was trying to find evidence to reopen the case around her uncle's suicide wouldn't endear her to the inspector.

"I see." Inspector Thorn's tone insinuated it couldn't be a coincidence that I was in the house the evening it was robbed. He swiveled on his heel and headed for the door. "Fingerprint boys will be along soon," he said over his shoulder. "I'll wait on those interviews, Lady Agnes, until after we get the results of the prints. I suggest you return to your beds and get some more sleep."

Boggs, who had been waiting at the door, cleared his throat. "Inspector, there is a broken window below stairs. Someone entered the house through the scullery."

Thorn's steps slowed, and he shot an irritated look at Boggs. "Fine. I'll take a look." Nunn hurried after the inspector, apparently intending to go with him to the scullery, but Thorn added, "Alone," which stopped Nunn in his tracks. "Go on, back to your rooms, all of you." Thorn flicked his hand as if a fly were pestering him. "I don't want any interference with my *crime scene*." He motioned for Boggs to lead the way downstairs.

CHAPTER TEN

I knew I'd never be able to go back to sleep, so when I returned to my room, instead of crawling into bed, I sat down at the writing desk. Normally, if I'm antsy and left to my own devices, I'll read. I always bring a book when visiting grand homes, and I'd brought two crime novels Jasper had recommended, but I wouldn't be able to get past the first page.

I took out a blank sheet of writing paper from the desk and listed everything that had happened since I'd met with Lady Agnes. I jotted down snatches of conversation and bits of information that stood out to me about each person. I also put down all the details Lady Agnes and Gilbert had given me about the morning Lord Mulvern's death had been discovered. I finished up by making a list of people who'd been present at the dinner party the night before Lord Mulvern died, and the questions I wanted to ask them. I'd already spoken briefly to Nora and Gilbert, and I felt it would be a waste of my time to ask them further questions. They'd told me all they would. I'd wait until I had more information before approaching them again. I did want to speak to the valet, Hodges, along with Nunn and Rathburn. Perhaps I would seek out Nunn and Hodges that morning.

I folded my notes and tucked them away in my handbag, then I selected a russet-colored day dress with black braid edging the cuffs and collar. I didn't bother to call for Martha. I was quite able to take care of myself. Inspector Thorn had not struck me as a man who would linger over the examination of the thief's entry point. I felt sure Thorn had only glanced around the room to appease Lady Agnes. I, on the other hand, was quite curious about this theft. Of course, the theft and the damage to the mummy might be completely unrelated to Lord Mulvern's death, but I intended to make sure I knew everything about it I could . . . just in case.

Once I was presentable, I went in search of the back staircase. The house was quiet, with only the servants moving wraithlike through the rooms as they cleaned and scrubbed and prepared for the day. I went through the green baize door and down the stairs to the floor below ground level, following the smell of warm bread.

The kitchen was warm and bustling with activity. My hunch that Thorn had departed was correct. Neither he nor any police officers were in the kitchen. Silence fell and motion ceased when the servants caught sight of me. The cook said to one of the kitchen maids, "Mind the toast, Junie," and broke the spell.

The housekeeper came forward, her keys jangling

against her skirt. "Miss Belgrave, good morning. I'm Mrs. Ryan. How can I help you?" she asked, her tone indicating I shouldn't be in the kitchen in the first place, and she intended to get me out as soon as she possibly could.

"Good morning, Mrs. Ryan. Which way to the scullery? I'd like to take a peek at it, then I'll be on my way."

Mrs. Ryan's face didn't change, but her posture stiffened. "That's not—"

I lowered my voice and leaned closer to her. "A break-in is quite thrilling, don't you think? I have the most horrible curiosity. I'm afraid it's something I just can't quite master . . . " Better to let Mrs. Ryan think I was a featherbrained young woman intent on gossip than to give her the real reason for my request to see the scullery. Lady Agnes hadn't specifically instructed me to keep my search for information quiet from the staff, but I'd leave it to her to make them aware of it. I'd keep my motives hush-hush in the meantime.

A look of what might've been disapproval flashed across Mrs. Ryan's face, but she must have decided the fastest way to get rid of me was to let me see the scullery. "This way."

I followed her into a small room off the kitchen.

Two sinks were on the far side, on an outside wall. A window above them looked out at ground level and let in a stream of morning light. One of the panes near the lock had been broken, and glass shards littered the sinks and the raised wooden slats that the scullery maids stood on to keep their feet dry. Beyond the shattered window, the leaves of a shrub shifted in the breeze.

The window was small, but with it pushed up to its full height, a slender adult would be able to wiggle through. A cool breeze drifted through the broken pane along with the smell of damp earth. The thief had used the sinks as a stepping-stone. Smeared muddy footprints covered the porcelain, and a line of the mucky impressions trailed across the stone floor, growing fainter as they neared the door.

I stood beside one of the less smudged prints. It was considerably larger and wider than my foot, and it didn't have the curved silhouette of a woman's shoe. It was obvious people had hurried to and fro, smearing some of the prints, so it was difficult to see if there were any distinguishing marks in the soles of the shoes. "The inspector was in to look at this?" I asked Mrs. Ryan.

"Yes. We've already sent for the glazer. The window will be repaired before the morning is out."

I motioned to the footprints. "And the inspector also sent someone to photograph these?"

"Photographs? Why would he do that?"

Inspector Thorn wasn't taking the break-in seriously. "No reason," I murmured. A maid entered with a scrub brush and stopped short when she saw me. I said, "I'll get out of your way now."

I left the bustle of the kitchen and stepped through the baize door into the hush of the ground floor. My heels clicked loudly across the marble. Was the break-in a coincidence? Did it have anything to do with Lady Agnes's questions around her uncle's death?

Of course the break-in might be completely unrelated to Lord Mulvern's death. What had Lady Agnes said about the young man she'd been speaking to when I arrived? She'd said he was a collector and single-minded when it came to his hobby. He'd made her an offer. Did he want to buy the mummy? What was his name? Eli? No . . . Ernest. Ernest Dennett.

Perhaps instead of purchasing antiquities, Dennett had decided to acquire valuables in another way. But if he was a collector, wouldn't he want the whole mummy? Surely he wouldn't destroy it only for some amulets and jewelry? I'd have to ask Lady Agnes.

The cavernous room where we had dined the previous evening was empty, but the aroma of toast, bacon, and coffee drifted out of the nearby breakfast room. Unlike the formal Victorian dining room with its ruby-red damask wall covering, the breakfast room contained Sheraton furnishings and was painted a pale cream. A single delicate chandelier hung from a neoclassical ceiling medallion, and a pair of enormous oil paintings—seascapes depicting violent storms—hung over the sideboard. Bowls of mums in autumn colors were spaced along the table.

Boggs, now in his formal jacket and with his hair perfectly parted, was placing a coffee pot on the side-board. "Good morning, Boggs," I said and filled my plate. The morning post had arrived with a letter from Essie, and I read it as I ate. Essie was thrilled to hear from me and would be able to meet me. She would be at Lyons Corner House near Piccadilly Circus at noon.

I was just finishing my egg and toast when Lady Agnes arrived. "Ah, good morning, Miss Belgrave. Did you get any additional sleep after our early morning disturbance?"

"No, I didn't even attempt it."

Lady Agnes filled her plate and took a seat across the table from me. "Neither did I. I was too cross."

Boggs took up his position under one of the stormy paintings after serving Lady Agnes coffee, and I kept my voice down to make sure he couldn't overhear me. "Do you think the theft is related to your uncle's death?"

Lady Agnes lowered her fork to her plate. "I've been so incensed about what happened, I hadn't even considered that." She stared at the flower arrangement of bronze mums for a moment. "I don't *think* the two things are related, but I could be wrong."

"It does seem a bit strange that you'd have a break-in and the only things that were stolen were items from inside a mummy. I assume there are more valuable items in the grand gallery?"

"Without a doubt."

"Have you had other break-ins?"

"No. Never."

"Do you suppose . . . the man you said was interested in your collection—Mr. Dennett, wasn't it?—could he have had something to do with the break-in?"

"Mr. Dennett?" Lady Agnes shook her head immediately. "No, he's far too fussy for anything like that."

"And I suppose he'd rather have the whole mummy, not just the amulets and jewelry?"

Lady Agnes shook her head and spoke more slowly. "No, he doesn't care about the mummies themselves. I have no doubt that if he *acquired* the Zozar mummy, Mr.

Dennett would have the linen stripped off as soon as possible to get at the funerary ornaments." She took up her fork. "Let's see what the fingerprint evidence reveals. I don't want you to get sidetracked from Uncle Lawrence's death."

"I agree. I'd like to speak to everyone who attended the dinner party the evening before your uncle died. Since I've already spoken to your brother and sister-in-law, I'll tackle Mr. Nunn this morning."

"Excellent plan, except Mr. Nunn has a meeting first thing this morning, so he's unavailable."

"Then I'd better start with your uncle's valet."

"My thoughts exactly." Lady Agnes spread marmalade on her toast. "I wrote a note to Hodges and sent it off yesterday after we spoke. I assumed you'd want to talk with him. I wanted him to know you have my blessing to speak with him. I'll give you his direction, and you can visit him this morning."

"Thank you, I'll do that." Although it was exactly the plan I'd hoped to execute, I felt a little outmaneuvered because Lady Agnes had already anticipated my moves. Was I running this investigation or was she?

I bundled up in my coat and gloves and let myself out the front door since Boggs was still busy in the breakfast room. No footman was on duty in the entrance hall, but that wasn't surprising. Since the war, high society had cut back on staff, partly out of necessity—death duties were high—but also because fewer people were going into service.

I set out on foot because the day wasn't cloudy. Puddles dotted the grass, and I stayed on the paths as I made my way across Hyde Park. The leaves that had already fallen were a soggy mess, but the ones that remained on the trees flickered in shades of burnished copper, glowing gold, and deep russet.

Hodges lived in a modern service flat in a neighborhood not far from where I lived. The address of my boardinghouse might optimistically be considered on the very fringe of Belgravia. Hodges's neighborhood was a step up from mine. His flat was actually *in* Belgravia.

The hall porter was not on duty, and I went right up in the elevator to the fourth floor address Lady Agnes had given me. At my knock, a man in his late sixties opened the door. He had dark eyes under a heavy brow, and a wary manner.

"Mr. Hodges? I'm Olive Belgrave. Lady Agnes sent you a note about me coming around to visit you."

"Yes, I received it. Won't you come in?" While his words were correct and welcoming, his manner was stiff. Clearly, he'd only invited me in because Lady Agnes had asked and expected him to do so. If he'd had his choice, he wouldn't have opened the door in the first place.

Lionel Hodges was a distinguished man with salt-and-pepper hair swept back from a widow's peak. He was immaculately dressed from his perfectly knotted tie and dark gray suit down to his polished shoes. His standard of dress had certainly not fallen off since his retirement as a gentleman's gentleman.

I stepped into the hallway. It was so narrow I had to

take a few paces forward so he could close the door. Two doors opened off the end of the short passageway. He motioned to the door on the left. "Please, come into the sitting room. Can I offer you a cup of tea? I was just making a pot for Mother and me."

"Oh," I said. Lady Agnes hadn't mentioned his mother. Perhaps his mother was visiting? "Yes, that would be nice."

He escorted me into the room, a small but comfortably furnished space with a mix of modern streamlined furniture and heavy Victorian pieces. A lady with white hair as thin and fluffy as the fuzz around a dandelion sat in a rocker near the window. She looked up from her knitting as I entered the room behind Hodges.

"Mother, this is Miss Belgrave," he said. "She's come for a visit."

She smiled as she continued to knit. "How nice." Her expression seemed faintly welcoming, but there was also a vacancy about her gaze. She dipped her head and focused on the yarn.

Hodges said, "Please have a seat. I'll be back in a moment with the tea."

As I sank into the velvet-covered Victorian sofa, I said to Mrs. Hodges, "It's a lovely autumn day."

Mrs. Hodges's gaze went to the window. "Yes, yes it is. Always did love autumn. So much nicer than winter with dirty snow."

She returned her attention to her knitting. The needles clicked in a steady counterpoint to the creak of the rocking chair.

"That's a beautiful blue yarn," I said.

"Blue. Blue is my favorite color," she said without

lifting her gaze from her knitting. I'd thought she was knitting a scarf, but she shifted in her chair, and I saw her knitting trailed off her lap, down the side of the chair, and created an enormous puddle near her feet. She paused in her rocking and looked at me again. "Do you like blue?"

It seemed my answer was an extremely serious matter, so I matched her tone when I answered. "Yes, it's one of my favorite colors."

She resumed rocking. "Good." She gave a short nod, and I began to understand that her mental capacity was perhaps more similar to a child than an adult.

Hodges returned with a tray of tea and biscuits. "Here we are. Would you like to pour for us? Mother's hands are not quite as steady as they once were."

"I'd be delighted."

Hodges took the teacup I poured for his mother, added cream and sugar, and put a biscuit on the saucer. He placed it on a table near Mrs. Hodges. "Here you are, Mother, the tea you wanted."

"Tea?"

"Yes. Remember? You asked for it a little while ago."

Mrs. Hodges didn't reply. She nibbled on her biscuit and took a few sips of tea. Mr. Hodges took his own cup and settled into a chair across from me. "I suppose you're here because you want to know if I murdered Lord Mulvern."

My gaze shifted to Hodges's mother. She'd put down her tea and had gone back to her yarn. There was no break in the creak of her rocking chair or the clack of her needles.

Hodges said, "Don't mind Mother. She's . . . in her

own world, very much unaware of what goes on here. You can speak freely. Lady Agnes said you would have questions. I'm fully prepared to answer anything you ask me."

I was surprised Hodges had been so direct. I decided to be as bold, and a bit cheeky as well. "Did you? Murder Lord Mulvern?"

CHAPTER ELEVEN

My impertinent question must have hit the right note with Hodges. He gave me a small smile, and the set of his shoulders relaxed. "No, I did not murder Lord Mulvern," he said in amiable tones. "I held Lord Mulvern in great esteem—even considered him a friend. Besides, if I wanted to do away with him, there were plenty of ways for me to do it that wouldn't involve implicating myself."

"Such as?" I asked. It was obviously something he had thought about.

"A slip in the bath can be deadly." Then he gestured to his neck. "A jog of the hand when one is shaving is also rather dangerous."

What he said was true. Shaving razors were quite lethal. A shift of the hand and forceful pressure could cause quite a bit of damage and perhaps even be fatal. Drowning someone in a tub was another well-known murder method. All the newspaper articles about

George Smith had explained exactly how he'd killed his wives in the bath.

Hodges crossed one leg over the other. "I assure you, if I'd intended to kill Lord Mulvern, I certainly would have established a solid alibi for myself."

"That sounds incredibly reasonable, but there's still the fact that you inherited a large amount of money." I let my gaze travel around the room. "Enough to purchase a very comfortable modern flat."

Hodges looked at his mother and then back to me. "My mother is not quite . . . right in the head. It became apparent a few years ago she would need care and supervision—constant care. I went to Lord Mulvern, prepared to tender my resignation, but he offered a different solution." Hodges hesitated, then said, "This is strictly confidential. I'm only telling you because Lady Agnes has asked you to look into Lord Mulvern's death. If you have a full understanding of what happened, perhaps it will help Lady Agnes to under-stand. I left Mulvern House shortly after the will was read and didn't realize the extent of Lady Agnes's concern about her uncle's death."

"So Lord Mulvern had made some sort of arrange-ment with you for a pension?" I asked, to keep him on point.

"Yes. It was agreed on last summer. I would continue working through the end of this year to give him time to find my replacement. In January, when I left service, Lord Mulvern would settle a—um—significant amount of money on me, enough to purchase this flat. And then I was to have a pension as well."

"That was quite generous of him."

"It was." Hodges examined the nap of the fabric on his trousers. "I think Lord Mulvern also looked on me as a—well, you might say, a friend."

"You were in the war together?"

"Yes." He only said the one word, but it spoke volumes. If I had any cash to spare, I would have put it all on a bet that Hodges had been Lord Mulvern's batman. I only had a partial understanding of what life had been like for the soldiers during the Great War, but the camaraderie that developed during wartime would have made a strong bond between the two men.

"It was generous. Exceedingly so. That was one of the reasons there was the stipulation of secrecy about it."

"Lord Mulvern didn't want you to share this information with the household?"

"No, he was afraid it would cause problems."

I could see how that would be possible. If Lord Mulvern had decided to do a favor for a servant he was especially close to but didn't intend to make it a standard for every servant who worked for him, I could see why he'd prefer Hodges to keep it quiet.

Hodges leaned toward me, propping his elbow on the arm of the chair. "It would make no sense for me to kill Lord Mulvern. What would be the advantage of killing him when I would have exactly the same benefits a few months later?"

"And the police knew about this bequest?"

Hodges's face settled into a somber expression. "Detective Inspector Thorn spoke to the solicitors when the investigation was initially opened, but then the verdict came in. It was decided that Lord Mulvern had taken his own life, and that was the end of it."

I put my empty teacup on the table. "Mr. Hodges, Lady Agnes is convinced her uncle didn't take his own life. She's asked me to sort out the truth around his death. Will you help me? What do you think about his death?"

Hodges's large forehead creased with wrinkles as he shook his head. "I never believed it either. But who was I to question the police? Now, Lady Agnes, she has clout." A small smile turned up his lips. "If anyone can get to the bottom of Lord Mulvern's death, she can."

"Will you tell me what happened that evening?"

"Certainly." He sat up straight, and I had the feeling he was picturing himself entering the witness box. "It was a normal evening. Lord Mulvern had guests in to dine. Once he went down to the drawing room, I put away the clothes he'd worn earlier. I brushed his jacket and checked his shoes. Then I filled the pitcher with water from the tap in the bathroom down the hall, set out a tumbler, and filled it with water. After that, I went downstairs to retrieve the clean handkerchiefs that the maid had forgotten to bring upstairs earlier that day. I put the handkerchiefs away, then I spent the rest of the evening in the kitchen until Lord Mulvern rang. I went upstairs and helped him change out of his evening clothes."

"And what was his manner when you saw him after dinner?"

"He seemed as he always was. He wasn't a jolly or chipper man. His personality was more subdued, but he was quite content, I thought. He didn't seem upset or depressed. I asked him if it had been a good evening. He replied it went well. He told me he would want to wear his brown suit the next day, and I said, 'very good, sir.' I wished him a good evening and left him." Hodges paused, his frown deepening.

"And what happened in the morning?" I prompted.

"I went in with his morning tea, as I always did. He was usually awake but not always, so I wasn't surprised the room was still dark. I put the tray on the table, then went to open the drapes. Lord Mulvern would usually say something along the lines of 'good morning' or comment on the weather, but he was completely quiet. When I went to the bed, I realized something was wrong."

"Did you think he was ill?"

"Oh no. I knew from the moment I looked at him that he was gone. He wasn't breathing. His skin was as white as the porcelain in the bath, and his mouth was hanging open." Hodges cleared his throat. "I went and roused Mr. Gilbert straightaway."

"And he was in his room? Gilbert, I mean?"

"Yes. In his dressing room, that is. He and his wife had had a spat the night before." Disapproval crept into Hodges's tone as he mentioned Nora. "Mr. Gilbert always slept in the dressing room after one of their dust-ups."

"I suspect an argument between them wasn't unusual?"

"No, they fought all the time. Mostly about money." He stopped speaking suddenly and shifted in his chair, apparently remembering he was speaking of the family who had provided such a generous legacy for him.

"Mr. Hodges," I said, "I know it seems rather sordid to discuss these things, but I need to know everything that happened leading up to Lord Mulvern's death. Even the smallest detail could make a difference." I'd learned that what initially seemed insignificant could actually be of greatest importance.

Hodges let out a sigh. "I suppose it must be done. I do know they argued about money that evening. Mrs. Nora—Viscountess Clifton as she was then—had tried to talk Lord Mulvern into purchasing a flat for her and Mr. Gilbert, but Lord Mulvern refused."

"A flat of their own? But Mulvern House is so large and luxurious." It was hard to imagine a newlywed couple needing more room. Surely they could live quite comfortably in such a sumptuous town house.

"Oh yes. She was determined to have her own flat. Lord Mulvern was equally as determined he was not going to purchase one for them. He said if Mr. Gilbert wanted his own flat, Mr. Gilbert could get a job. But Mr. Gilbert didn't want his own flat. He was perfectly content to live at Mulvern House."

"Gilbert didn't have an allowance or an income of his own?" I asked. Many of my friends had no jobs, but they had plenty of money either from parents or from inheritances.

"Lord Mulvern gave Mr. Gilbert a generous allowance, but Mr. Gilbert is a spendthrift. And then after he married—well, then they went through each quarter's allowance twice as fast."

"Hmm," I murmured and tucked that bit of information away to contemplate later. I didn't want to get too far from the topic we'd been discussing.

"Going back to the morning you discovered Lord Mulvern had . . . *passed on,* did Nora also come to his room?"

"No, she was in the bedchamber which adjoins the dressing room where Mr. Gilbert slept. The door was closed between the two rooms, so she wouldn't have heard me summon Mr. Gilbert. Good, stout doors at Mulvern House, you know. We summoned the police and called the doctor."

"And the note? Did you see it?"

"Not until Lady Agnes spotted it. I didn't even notice it. Of course, it was dark in the room when I came in, and my attention had been on the bed, not the writing desk."

"Of course. And what did you think of the note?"

"Not much of a goodbye for his family, I thought, if you want to know the truth."

"I agree."

"I told the police all of this."

"I'm sure you did. I appreciate you going over it again with me. It's helpful to hear everyone's impressions firsthand. Was there anything else?"

He seemed to be on the verge of saying something, then drew back.

"Anything at all? A small detail, perhaps something that you thought of between that time and now?"

"I'm not even sure if it's correct," he said slowly. "Our minds are strange, and sometimes they play tricks on us." He glanced at his mother, whose scarf had grown by several inches since I'd arrived. "I can't be sure—I'm not positive at all—but when I returned with the clean handkerchiefs and stepped into the room, I thought there was the scent of a ladies' perfume in the air. I didn't remember it until I was in Selfridge's weeks later. I walked by the counter with the scent, and it all came back. At the time the police were asking questions, I didn't think of it at all."

"What was the scent?"

"Lily of the valley."

CHAPTER TWELVE

*a*s I made my way to Piccadilly Circus to meet Essie, I mulled over what Hodges had told me. He could have made up the detail about the scent of lily of the valley in Lord Mulvern's room, but Nora *had* been evasive when I'd spoken to her about the night Lord Mulvern had died. But was Nora so greedy she'd kill Lord Mulvern? His death did mean Gilbert inherited. A flat would be well within Gilbert's financial ability now. Why did Gilbert and Nora continue to live at Mulvern House? Perhaps as the lady of the house, Nora was satisfied with her position now and didn't want to move?

After a second's consideration, I brushed that thought away. Nora didn't seem the least bit interested in the duties of the mistress of Mulvern House. She'd only remembered approving the dinner menu when Lady Agnes had prompted her, and the servants continued to consult Lady Agnes. It wasn't the social position Nora wanted, which only left one reason for

Nora to kill her father-in-law—the money Gilbert would inherit.

I was so lost in my thoughts, I nearly walked by Lyon's Corner House, but I came out of my reverie and hurried through the food hall on the ground floor, barely glancing at the pastries, chocolates, cheese, wine, and flowers. I went upstairs to the crowded restaurant. Essie wore distinctive hats, so she was easy to find. A quick scan, and I spotted her. In the past, she'd favored wide-brimmed tricorn hats, but apparently she'd embraced the cloche. She wore a gray and black felt hat designed like a tube, which nearly covered her nose, but I could still see her pink cheeks and rounded face. I was wearing a cloche as well, but mine was more modest in size, only covering my forehead and ears.

I reached her table and bent down to peer under the brim. "Essie, are you inside that drainpipe?"

"You're too funny, Olive," Essie said, taking my comment as the joke it was meant to be. "It's the latest thing. You'll have one next week, I assure you."

"I doubt it." I pulled out a chair. "I can't afford it, for one thing."

"Really? Even with your recent successes?"

"Rent, darling. You know how it is."

"And food—the prices are simply outrageous," Essie said, then ordered the four-course luncheon.

I ordered the same but added a slice of cake. A girl could never have too much cake. I might not be able to splurge on a new hat, but I could afford a piece of chocolate cake.

Essie took out a notebook and pen from her handbag. "Now, what do you have for me?"

"A question."

Essie shook her head. "No, Olive. That's what *I* ask *you*."

"Later, I promise." I leaned over the table. I had to go carefully here. Essie could pick up on the tiniest bit of gossip and blow it up into a newspaper headline if I wasn't careful. "These articles in *The Hullabaloo* about the mummy—who's the source of information?"

"No idea, and old Charlie Crimpton won't let on a word about where he's getting the stories." Essie slapped her pen down. "It's frightfully annoying. All the good assignments go to Charlie and Henry and . . . well, all the other boys. Anything to do with Lord Mulvern should go on the society page. All those stories should be mine."

"Hmm. Are you sure you couldn't find out?" Before she could ask why, I hurried on. "I have an invite to the opening night of the Egyptian exhibit that the Mulvern family is sponsoring at the British Museum. If you can find out who the source is, I'll give you all the details about the opening night—an exclusive."

Essie tilted her head. "Why?"

Trust Essie to get right to the point. "I can't tell you right now, but you'll be the first—and only one—to know the whole story when I can tell it."

Essie toyed with her pen. "Well, you have been rather successful in the past."

"And I gave you the scoop in both cases. Inside access to a big story—so big you might be able to write about crime instead of society news."

"In that case, give me a day. Old Charlie won't know what hit him."

~

I walked back to Mulvern House, confident that if there was a way for Essie to wrangle the information out of her colleague at the newspaper, she'd do it. She was relentless when she was pursuing a story. Rather like I was when I was after the truth, I realized. The thought caused me to slow my steps. I'd never considered that I might be similar to Essie in any way. I could be single-minded, but I hoped I was determined, not obstinate.

I'd intended to turn at the side street that ran along the west side of the house and make my way to the front door, but I noticed a man in a bowler hat and brown suit leave the servants' entrance. I probably wouldn't have given him another glance except he paused and looked over his shoulder at the house as he trotted up the servants' steps, a furtive movement that caught my attention. It was Boggs.

He scanned the street. I hadn't turned the corner yet, and a woman pushing a pram stopped and adjusted a blanket, shielding me from his view. Boggs turned away and set off at a brisk pace. I watched him for a moment, then followed him but kept back. If he turned around, I wouldn't be directly behind him. Perhaps following him was foolish, and it might not amount to anything. But I'd always been one to go with my instincts, and my intuition told me Boggs didn't want anyone to know where he was going. Therefore, he was probably going somewhere interesting.

Boggs wasn't out for a random stroll. His pace was speedy, and he moved with purpose along the pavement. I had to dash along behind him to keep up. We left the polished door knockers and freshly washed steps of Mayfair. The neighborhoods gradually transitioned to a grittier area, where he turned into a shop with grimy windows and peeling paint on the trim.

I switched to a leisurely pace, barely moving along the pavement. I was afraid Boggs might pop out of the door and into my path, but the shop door remained closed. I inched forward. It was an antiques shop. Through the dirty glass, I saw Boggs was at the far side of the shop with his back to me as he talked with a man behind a counter. I took a deep breath and turned the knob.

Bells jangled as I stepped inside. I spun around so my back was to the two men and closed the door. I was glad I'd worn my cloche. It wasn't as concealing as Essie's hat had been, but I didn't worry that Boggs would recognize me straightaway if he happened to glance. I drifted to the far side of the shop and bent over a glass display case containing pocket watches. The conversation between the two men carried on without a pause, but not loud enough that I could hear their words. I gradually moved through the shop, pausing to admire a silver tea set.

A mummy case propped against the wall in the back caught my eye. I worked my way deeper into the shop, weaving through tables with lamps, musical instruments, Chinese boxes, sea shells, and clocks. I stopped in front of the mummy case. The vermillion, gold, and lapis decoration stood out even in the low light at the back of the shop. Now that I was closer, the men's voices became distinct.

". . . you got for me today, old man?" asked the man

on the other side of the counter, placing a mocking emphasis on the last two words.

I risked a glance over my shoulder. Boggs was still positioned with his back to me, but I could see the face of the man on the other side of the counter. He was younger than Boggs, probably in his mid-thirties, and wore a suit with a flashy yellow waistcoat.

"I've got nothing for you today," Boggs said, "except a warning. If you had anything to do with the break-in at Mulvern House, you'll regret it."

I was stunned at the rough edge of Boggs's voice. His refined accent had vanished, and his tone was aggressive.

The other man laughed, a wheezy gasp that didn't sound healthy. "Break-in? So the grand house has been robbed, has it?"

"Are you saying you had nothing to do with it?"

"Course not." The man's raspy laugh trailed off. "I don't get involved in foolishness like that. You forget I'm an upstanding businessman now."

I shifted to look at the wares beside the mummy. Shock jolted through me as I realized the pieces on display were parts of mummies. Little tags identified the bundles as *mummy hand* and *mummy foot*. There were even a couple of mummified heads. My stomach churned a bit, and I turned away. How odd—and disrespectful—to cut up a mummy. Who would do that?

The proprietor raised his voice. "Looking for anything in particular, miss?"

I pitched my voice higher and kept my face turned away from the men as I replied, "No, I just wandered in for a quick browse." I drifted a couple of steps back toward the shop door.

The owner dropped his voice to speak to Boggs. "I got customers. Shove off."

I tilted my head and watched the two men out of the corner of my eye. "If you hear anything about that robbery," Boggs said, then pushed his finger into the other man's chest as he spoke the last four words, "you let me know."

The other man swatted his hand away. "Oh, so they'd like their things back—even if they have to buy them?"

"Just contact me if you hear anything." Boggs wheeled around, and I ducked, pretending to examine a Roman bust of Caligula. Boggs swept past me. The bells jangled, and the door banged.

I could feel the proprietor moving in my direction, and I resumed my falsetto tones. "Lovely items you have here, but I'm afraid I have an appointment." I moved to the door before the man could get a look at my face.

The bells tinkled as I stepped outside and scanned the street. Boggs was heading back in the direction he'd come at his relentless pace. It was only as I turned away from the shop that I noticed the gold lettering on the window. *Antiquities, jewelry, and other fine items. S. Boggs, Proprietor.*

CHAPTER THIRTEEN

trailed Boggs back to Mulvern House, keeping well back. He plowed on without a backward glance, and I mulled over whether or not I should tell Lady Agnes what I'd seen. It had nothing to do with her uncle's death . . . did it? And if her butler was perhaps the grandfather or older uncle of an antique shop owner, that didn't necessarily mean Boggs had a hand in the theft of the antiquities. I wouldn't toss out baseless accusations about Boggs, but I could let Lady Agnes know she should double check her butler's references.

I was a few blocks from the turn that would take me to Mulvern House when a newsboy shouted, "Curse strikes again! The mummy's curse is real. The curse continues!"

I picked up my pace, closing the distance between myself and the newsboy as I dug in my handbag for some coins. The story was on the front page of *The*

Hullabaloo and again featured oversized capital letters, this time reading, *MUMMY CURSE WON'T DIE*.

The article contained the gist of the events of the previous night—the theft of the amulets from inside the mummy—but it was embellished with fabricated details about strange moaning sounds and ghostly apparitions that made for much more entertaining reading. A small photograph of a mummy accompanied the article, but it must've been an image the newspaper already had in its files. It looked nothing like the scene from the night before.

I folded the newspaper and tucked it under my arm as I moved between the gates of Mulvern House. Who was feeding this information to the papers? A servant? Perhaps someone on the police force? One of the family? I hoped Essie could find out. I couldn't explain why, but I felt that the leaks to the newspaper and the break-in were all tied up together with Lord Mulvern's death.

A footman opened the door. As I stepped inside, I said, "Good afternoon. Where is Boggs?"

"He has the afternoon off, miss."

"I see."

"He should be back shortly, if you have need of him."

I left my coat with a footman and drew off my gloves as I went upstairs. I met Nora and another woman coming down. We paused on the landing where the staircase split, and Nora waved a languid hand, introducing me to her friend, Dorothy Gill, saying, "Miss Belgrave is staying with us a few days."

Dorothy reached for my hand and pumped it. "*Such* a pleasure to meet you, Miss Belgrave." She was brimming with enthusiasm from her wide brown eyes to the curls that bounced on either side of her face. She reminded me of a puppy looking for a ball to chase, full of boundless, undirected energy. "I can't tell you how much I admire you." She put a hand to her flat chest. "I can't imagine staying here overnight—not with a mummy haunting the place." She shivered—with delight, I thought—and gripped Nora's forearm. "Of course, I'd do it for you, Nora. I'm sure it would be terribly frightening, but I'd stay if you wanted me to," she said with a hint of pleading.

"That's all nonsense, Dorothy. No need to be so dramatic about it." Nora's reply was like a douse of cold water.

Dorothy removed her hand. "Oh—but the newspapers . . . and you said you were frightened—"

Nora clamped her hand above Dorothy's elbow. "Sorry, Miss Belgrave, but we absolutely must be going or I'll miss my appointment with the dressmaker," she said as she propelled Dorothy down the stairs.

"So happy to have met you, Miss Belgrave. I hope we're able to chat longer next time," she said over her shoulder.

"Yes, I hope so, too."

In my room, I tossed my gloves, the newspaper, and my handbag into an armchair. I took off my hat and turned to the dressing table for a comb. A white envelope with my name was propped against the glass of the dressing table. It was a heavy white paper with a slight nap to it like the plain writing paper in my desk. I didn't recognize the handwriting, which was rather blocky.

I ripped open the envelope and took out a single sheet paper that was of the same quality as the envelope. Hieroglyphs covered the sheet—birds, figures of people, lines, and circles. I went to find Lady Agnes or Nunn. I supposed either one of them could tell me what it said.

Lady Agnes was in the morning room. I hesitated on the threshold. She was at the desk by the window and held the earpiece of the telephone to her ear. She saw me and motioned for me to come in. ". . . yes, that will be acceptable. Thank you." She dropped the receiver back into the cradle as she turned to me. "Hello, Miss Belgrave. I can't tell you how glad I am to have a telephone installed in here. Uncle Lawrence hated the things and refused to have one in his study, so I said to run the line in here instead. It's saved me bundles of time."

"I don't want to interrupt," I said.

"Nonsense. I'm finished with what I was working on. Come in. I'm anxious to hear how you're getting on. Have you made any progress?"

"Possibly." There were fewer crates and boxes scattered around the room today, and I didn't have to take an undulating path through them to get to the chair she motioned to. I handed her the paper. "I found this in my room. Perhaps you can tell me what it says? Or should I look for Mr. Nunn?"

Lady Agnes seemed a bit distracted as she pushed the telephone to the back corner of her desk and closed a folder. She gave the paper a quick glance as she took it from me, then she went still. "No—there's no need to find Mr. Nunn."

Her voice had changed. It held a seriousness that hadn't been there a moment earlier.

"What does it say?"

She looked at me a moment, seeming to weigh her words. "I'm afraid it's a warning—a rather nasty one—from one of the tombs."

"Oh my. A curse?"

"Some people call them curses, but they're really warnings. They typically have a formula. If a certain action is taken, then something bad will befall the person who took that action. This one just contains the last part of the warning, the punishment."

"What does it say?"

She hesitated again, then said, "It actually contains two warnings. *I shall seize his neck like that of a goose.*" She glanced at me to see how I was taking it.

"Go on. What's the rest?"

"*And he shall not exist.*" She rotated her shoulders. "They're from completely different dynasties. Sloppy scholarship," she said, and I thought she was trying to add a light note to the rather dire pronouncements.

"Well, that's excellent," I said. "And I thought I wasn't making much progress at all. Rather creepy, but overall it's a very good sign."

"I'm sorry?"

"I thought I hadn't found anything significant, but someone is nervous enough to warn me off, which is progress."

She handed the paper back to me. "I see. I'd say

'congratulations,' but that doesn't seem appropriate."
She gave me a small smile. "I'll settle for 'carry on.'"

"I intend to. Is Mr. Nunn available now?"

"I believe so."

"Good. I'll speak to him before lunch, then I'll drop in on Rathburn." I headed for the door, then turned back. "How did you come to hire Boggs?"

"He came to us through our usual agency. Why? Is something wrong?"

"I'm not sure, but it might be useful to double check his references."

"You think—?"

"No. I don't have anything except suppositions. He was the only person to join your staff shortly before your uncle died. You said everyone else has been with you for years and years. It couldn't hurt to double check Boggs."

She swiveled her chair back to her desk, opened a drawer, and removed a file. "Fredrick Boggs," she read, "worked for the Misses Piedmont in Northumberland before coming to us. I'll write to them today."

"I think that's a good idea." I moved to the door, but it opened before I could reach it. Boggs came in with a letter on a salver. He was back in his formal black suit. He held the door for me. His usual impassive glance was missing. Instead, I felt his gaze burning into my shoulder blades as I left the room.

CHAPTER FOURTEEN

The smooth lines of the pink granite statue of Ramses II loomed over me. Only the head and shoulders of the figure had survived from antiquity, and I found it hard to imagine what the complete sculpture would have looked like. Gargantuan, I imagined. I took a few steps to the side, and the click of my heels on the polished floor echoed around the empty gallery in the British Museum.

Currently, I had the room to myself. I hadn't been able to talk to Nunn. He'd stepped out again, so I'd left for my meeting with Rathburn. When I'd arrived at the museum, I'd expected to be taken to a corridor lined with offices, but the young man on duty had told me Rathburn was delayed and would meet me in the Egyptian Galleries. That had been at least a quarter of an hour before. While I didn't like being kept waiting, I certainly couldn't complain about the opportunity to view the antiquities.

A scuffling sound came from behind me, and I turned. Even though the man was on the opposite side of the large room, Rathburn's shock of white hair and beard made him easy to recognize. He looked like a portly Father Christmas in a dark suit as he waddled around a pedestal, except that when he was closer, I could see his expression was one of impatience instead of holiday jolliness.

"Good afternoon, Miss Belgrave. Lady Agnes said you had a question for me?"

"Quite a few, actually. Is there somewhere we could go? Perhaps your office?"

Rathburn took out a pocket watch, which was attached to a gold chain that stretched across his rotund stomach. "I'm afraid I only have a few moments to spare."

Irritation bristled through me.

He snapped the watch closed. "I understand it's regarding the late Lord Mulvern."

I'd rather have sat down with Rathburn, but I'd have to make the best of the situation. I tamped down my annoyance. "I'll get right to the point, then. What can you tell me about the dinner party Lord Mulvern hosted the night before he died?"

"The food was excellent, as always. Dinners always are at Mulvern House. The pudding was outstanding. A new recipe, I believe Lady Agnes said."

"No, I meant what was the atmosphere of the dinner party?"

Rathburn's bushy white eyebrows rose. "The atmosphere?"

"Was it an amiable gathering? Was there tension in the air?"

"No, it was just . . ." He waved a plump hand. ". . . a normal evening. We had drinks before dinner, we dined, and then we had coffee in the drawing room."

"What did you converse about?"

He stroked his beard. "The upcoming exhibit, I believe. Can't remember any specific details."

"I see."

And I did indeed. Rathburn wasn't going to give anything away. I didn't buy for one moment that he didn't remember anything about the dinner party except the food.

"Did anyone leave the group during the evening?"

"Leave?"

I squashed a sigh at having to repeat all my questions. "Did you notice anyone slip out?"

"Can't say that I did. I know *I* stayed with the group all evening."

"That's interesting. Gilbert said you were apart from the group between the time the men left the dining room and entered the drawing room."

Pink tinged Rathburn's cheeks above his beard. "That's irrelevant. I never left the first floor."

Goodness—I realized I'd embarrassed him as he continued to sputter. "I—I only—a young woman such as yourself shouldn't concern herself with things like that." He consulted his watch again. "Now, I must leave you here. But please, enjoy the galleries for as long as you like."

He shuffled off at a faster pace than he'd approached me. I watched his squat figure depart, thinking it was amazing how he lost his tendency to verboseness when the subject was Lord Mulvern's last dinner party. Had the questions I'd tried to ask him at dinner caused him to write a note of hieroglyphic warnings? He certainly had the ability to compose such a note, and since he was so fond of bribes, he could pay one of the servants to put it in my room.

I was about to turn away when a man in a Homburg hat and gray suit came through the door at the other end of the gallery. Rathburn greeted him, and I realized it was Ernest Dennett, the man who'd been speaking to Lady Agnes when I first met her. I recognized his close-set eyes and slight build. He clasped his hands together behind his back, and Rathburn tucked his thumbs into his waistcoat pockets. The two men strolled off without a look at the antiquities surrounding them, their heads bent toward each other.

When I arrived at Mulvern House, Boggs was back at the door. He didn't seem to give me any more attention than he normally would, but with butlers, it's difficult to discern any of their emotions.

After dropping my hat, gloves, and handbag in my room—I was glad to see the dressing table was free of any new anonymous notes—I went directly to Nunn's office. It was adjacent to the library and must have originally been a storage area because the room had no windows. Filing cabinets lined one wall of the small room while floor-to-ceiling bookshelves with leather-bound volumes filled the rest of the room. Nunn was bent over the desk, but when I tapped on the door, he put down his pen and stood, pushing his spectacles up the bridge of his nose. "Please come in, Miss Belgrave. Lady Agnes told me you wished to speak to me. I'm sorry I wasn't in earlier."

"That's all right, Mr. Nunn," I said. "I'm sure you're extremely busy." Books always attracted my attention, and I skimmed the titles. Most were related to archeology or Egypt.

Nunn noticed my gaze roving over the volumes. He motioned to the shelves. "Overflow from the library next door. Lord Mulvern—the previous Lord Mulvern—had bookshelves installed here as his collection grew."

"Clever. Although, it looks as if you've almost run out of room here." Only a few shelves near the ceiling were empty.

"I think the acquisition of books will slow down now with the new Lord Mulvern. He's not a scholar."

"What about Lady Agnes? She shares her uncle's interest in archeology."

"She's much more of a doer than a reader," he said as he indicated one of the leather club chairs in front of his desk.

"Yes, I can see that about her." I took a seat. "Thank you for taking the time to talk to me."

"I'm happy to help. If you'll just give me a moment . . ." He picked up his fountain pen and signed *G. Wilfred Nunn* in a flourish so large I could read it from the other side of the desk. He set the letter aside and capped the pen. "Lady Agnes said you had questions about Lord Mulvern's death?" His face was blank, but there was something guarded in his tone as he shuffled papers marked with long columns and tidy checkmarks beside each item.

"Yes. Let's start with the dinner party the evening before Lord Mulvern's death. You were there?"

Did he look relieved when I mentioned the dinner party? I thought his face relaxed slightly, but it was hard to tell. He did stop tapping the edges of the papers into alignment and set them aside. "Yes, I always dine with the family when I'm here."

"Does your work take you away from Mulvern House frequently?" I asked, curious about how wide-ranging his responsibilities were, and I hoped the innocuous question would put him at ease.

"Yes, Lord Mulvern often sent me to meet with other collectors when he was interested in acquiring their pieces. I've also just completed an inventory at Lord Mulvern's country estate."

"I see. It must be interesting work."

"Fascinating." He glanced at an open ledger on one corner of the desk and inched the paper with the columns into position in front of him.

Since he seemed to want to get back to work, I said, "Tell me about the dinner party that evening."

Nunn picked up a pencil and rolled it back and forth between his palms. "I'm not sure what you mean."

"What did you discuss at dinner? What was the atmosphere like?"

"You've met Mr. Rathburn and dined with him. It was exactly like that." Irritation cracked through his blank façade.

"Mr. Rathburn told more of his stories?"

"To the point that the only thing that was discussed at dinner was Mr. Rathburn. His travel to Egypt was the only topic of conversation that evening."

"What were the interactions among the rest of the dinner party?"

"I don't remember much of anything except Mr. Rathburn droning on and on."

"And after dinner?"

"Coffee in the drawing room, as usual."

"Did anyone leave the dining room or the drawing room?"

"I don't think so. At least—" The smooth movement of his hands around the pencil halted, but then it resumed as he shook his head. "No, we were together all evening."

"You're sure," I asked.

"Yes," he said with confidence, but his gaze slipped away from mine.

"What time did Mr. Rathburn leave?"

"No idea. Sometime after we had coffee in the drawing room. Possibly around ten?"

"Did anyone accompany him to the door?"

"No. Boggs saw him out."

"Did you go into Lord Mulvern's room that evening?"

"No," he said. "Lord Mulvern conducted his business either in his study or in here."

"I see. And the next morning? Were you there when Hodges raised the alarm?"

"No." His wooden expression eased. "I had to meet a courier at the train station and examine his delivery."

A tap sounded, and we both turned to the door. A

maid said, "Begging your pardon, sir. Miss. There's a delivery here for Lord Mulvern, and the man insists you must sign for it personally, Mr. Nunn."

"Delivery?"

"Yes.

"Cabinetry, he says."

The pencil clattered onto the desk and rolled off the edge. Nunn scrambled to pick it up, slammed it down on the desk, and stood in one jerky movement. "I'll be there directly."

He turned to me. "I'm sorry, Miss Belgrave, but I must see to this. Perhaps we could continue the discussion later . . . ?"

"Yes, of course."

Nunn waited for me to precede him out of the room, a nervous energy radiating from him. As soon as I cleared the doorway and turned, his footsteps sprinted away in the opposite direction.

I went to the main floor and let myself out through the front door, then walked around to the side of the house to the service entrance at the back. I paused in the shadow of the building. A lorry with *McAllister's Cabinetry* on the side had pulled up to the door, blocking a lane of traffic. A man in a flat cap, rough trousers, and a heavy jacket that hung loosely off his large frame pounded his finger against a piece of paper. "But the toff ordered them. You can't just reject them."

Nunn must have run his fingers through his hair because unruly waves had sprung up around his face. He stood with one hand on his hip and the other across his mouth as he shook his head. He removed his hand

and pointed to the paper. "That order was canceled. Weeks ago."

"I don't see nothing here about any cancellation. We made the cabinets to order. Museum quality. You can't refuse delivery of a special order."

A squeak cut through the air from the back of the lorry, then a large glass display case came into view and rolled smoothly toward Nunn. The case swiveled, revealing another laborer pushing the wheeled dolly the case rested on. "Where'd you want it, gov'nor?"

Nunn flapped his hand. "Nowhere. Put it back. This is all wrong."

The first man shook the paper at Nunn. "We have a delivery, and we'll deliver it."

Nunn ran a hand through his hair, disarranging it further. "It was canceled, I tell you. *Canceled*. And it wasn't to be sent here at all. It was supposed to go to the British Museum."

The man balancing the dolly stroked the dark wood cabinet. "So these were for the exhibit. I remember now. The gentleman's donation."

Nunn made a shooing motion. "No. None of that's happening now. These must go back."

The three men were so immersed in their conversation, they didn't notice me as I slipped by and moved to the back of the lorry, which was open. Stacks of glass display cases filled the interior like those I'd seen at the museum. Some of the blankets that swaddled the cases had slipped, revealing glossy wood trim and panes of glass that reflected the sunlight.

The shriek of the dolly wheels announced the return of the laborer with the cabinet. He rounded the back of the lorry, shaking his head and muttering about 'toffs who didn't know anything.'

"These are for a donation?" I asked.

The man lowered the cabinet gently to the ground, took off his cap, and scratched his hairline. "They were. Lord Mulvern came to the shop and requested this mahogany." The man rubbed the grain of the wood trim. "He picked it out special, he did. It couldn't be anything ordinary since it was going to hold his collection when he gave it to the museum."

"You thought he was donating his collection to the British Museum?"

"Didn't think—*know*. Heard them talk about it myself. He was extremely particular. Had to be just right because it would house his collection for future generations—that's what he said." He pointed his thumb over his shoulder toward the front of the lorry, where Nunn was still talking with the first man. "No matter what that lad says, the gentleman ordered it for his donation."

"You heard Lord Mulvern specifically mention he was donating a portion of his collection to the British Museum?" I asked to make sure I understood correctly. This was the first I'd heard of anything like this, and if it was true . . . well, it put everything about Lord Mulvern's death in a new light.

"I heard him myself. He had a long chat with Mr. McAllister. I was working right beside them, setting the glass in a cabinet. There were no question about it. He was donating his collection. And not a little section of it. No, the entire thing."

"The entire collection?"

"Yes, ma'am. Rush order. That's why we're here today."

An engine rumbled, and I turned to see another lorry trundling up to us. The man put his cap back on. "Here's the rest of it."

CHAPTER FIFTEEN

"*I* don't believe it," Lady Agnes said as she paced back and forth across the carpet in her office. She'd asked me to pour the tea, which I was doing despite the fact that no one seemed interested in a cup.

The commotion outside Mulvern House, which had played out under the windows of Lady Agnes's office, had drawn her attention, and she'd come downstairs while the lorry drivers were arguing with Nunn. It had only taken Lady Agnes a few minutes to sort things out.

She'd taken the invoice from them and sent the lorry drivers on their way, telling them Mr. McAllister would be paid, but only after she verified the charges. Her voice held a note of authority that Nunn's didn't. The lorry drivers had climbed behind their steering wheels as Boggs stood in the street to halt traffic.

I set Lady Agnes's cup on a side table, but she didn't notice. She spun and faced Nunn, who was standing uncomfortably in the center of the room alternately smoothing his hair down and pushing his glasses up the bridge of his nose, looking like a child who had been called into the headmaster's office. Lady Agnes said, "It's impossible. Utterly impossible. Uncle Lawrence would never part with his collection."

Nunn tugged at his collar. "Begging your pardon, my lady, but it was true. He'd spoken to Mr. Rathburn about it—several times, in fact."

"Mr. Nunn." I held out a tea cup.

He glanced uncertainly at Lady Agnes.

"Oh, have a seat, Mr. Nunn. I'm too agitated to sit."

Nunn took the cup and perched on the edge of a chair, his gaze on Lady Agnes as she circled the room. Lapis was draped on top of the wingback chair, her head turning as she followed Lady Agnes around the room. On Lady Agnes's second circuit, the cat leapt down and landed lightly, then set off, tail held straight in the air and ears pricked up, following in Lady Agnes's wake.

"Perhaps Lord Mulvern wanted to make all the arrangements before telling you," Nunn said, his voice tentative.

"But Uncle Lawrence always discussed everything with me." Her words were argumentative but edged with hurt too. "We talked about where to dig, about which antiquities would go on display in the grand gallery, even about whether or not to hire *you*, Mr. Nunn. So I don't see why he would have overlooked mentioning to me he intended to donate his *entire collection* to the British Museum."

Nunn's Adam's apple bobbed as he swallowed. "All

I know is Lord Mulvern said everything had to be done with the strictest confidence. He only spoke to Mr. Rathburn about it, as far as I know."

"Mr. Rathburn!" Lady Agnes paced faster, and Lapis's paws skimmed over the carpet at her heels. "Uncle Lawrence wouldn't give his collection to Mr. Rathburn. Uncle Lawrence thought Mr. Rathburn was a fool."

"Perhaps your uncle was taking a longer view," said a male voice from the doorway. Lady Agnes stopped pacing, and Lapis disappeared under the desk.

Ernest Dennett stood in the doorway. I recognized his Homburg hat, his perfectly tailored suit, and his close-set green eyes. I'd seen him earlier that day speaking to Rathburn in the British Museum.

Boggs stood at the door. He cleared his throat. "Mr. Dennett, my lady."

"Oh! I'm sorry, Mr. Dennett," Lady Agnes said with a glance at the carriage clock on the mantle. "I completely forgot our appointment."

Dennett flicked a hand and said in his soft-spoken tones, "The National Gallery can wait. It seems there's much more exciting things going on here at Mulvern House."

"You know all about it, I suppose." Lady Agnes turned to me. "Mr. Dennett has a way of ferreting out all sorts of interesting information."

"My dear, the whole street knows what happened. With two enormous lorries blocking traffic while their vocal drivers converse loudly, you could expect nothing less. The news will be all over London before dinner."

Lady Agnes sighed. "I'm sure you're right." She

introduced me to Mr. Dennett. His gaze ran over me as she spoke, and I knew he was assessing the quality of my frock and shoes. "Pleasure to meet you," he said in an offhanded manner, then returned his attention to Lady Agnes.

She pushed her curls behind her ears and gestured to the sofa, where she took a seat. "Do sit down and join us for tea."

As I poured a cup for Dennett, Lady Agnes picked up her cup, brought it halfway to her mouth, then replaced it in the saucer. "What did you mean about Uncle Lawrence taking the long view, Mr. Dennett?"

"Only that Mr. Rathbun will not be with the British Museum forever." Dennett added five lumps of sugar to his tea and topped it off with a heavy dollop of cream, raising the level of the liquid nearly to the brim. "The museum is a distinguished institution, and Mr. Rathburn is only the first in what I'm sure will be a long line of Keepers of the Egyptian and Assyrian Collection. Perhaps your uncle realized his collection would have the most prominence at the British Museum. It's all about longevity."

Lady Agnes's curls trembled as she shook her head. "I don't believe that for a moment." She shifted her chair and pinned her gaze on Nunn. "Surely there's some other explanation."

Nunn choked on his tea, and I didn't blame him. I wouldn't want to be the focus of Lady Agnes's attention when she was cross.

"I can't speak to Lord Mulvern's motivation," Nunn said. "All I know is that he had several conversations with Mr. Rathburn. He visited Mr. McAllister's shop, and then he told me to order the cabinets."

"But why didn't you mention those things to Lady Agnes or her brother after Lord Mulvern passed away?" I asked. I had a good idea why he kept quiet about it, but I wanted to see his reaction.

His Adam's apple surged up and down. "Lord Mulvern's death was so sudden and such a painful topic, it seemed better to wait . . . a *decent* amount of time before I brought it up. The less said, the better, I thought."

"And so you canceled the order for the cabinetry?" Lady Agnes asked sharply.

He squirmed in his chair. "Well, yes. I knew nothing had been settled as far as the donation went, so I contacted the cabinetry firm and stopped the order. It had to be done, or . . ."

"They would complete the order and arrive with it," Lady Agnes said. "And when did you plan on telling me about the donation?"

"Oh—well, I didn't have an exact date. In the future . . ."

"I see," Lady Agnes said, and Nunn shifted again under her stare. "And do you know of any other projects or plans Uncle Lawrence was keeping secret?"

"No," Nunn said quickly, obviously relieved to be on a subject he felt more comfortable with. "The donation was the only thing of that kind."

"Do you have any other invoices or paperwork related to Uncle Lawrence's mad scheme?"

"A few notes he had me take down after one of his meetings with Mr. Rathburn."

"Then retrieve them, Mr. Nunn. I want to see them."

Nunn's cup clattered against the saucer as he shoved it onto the tea tray and hurried out of the room.

Lady Agnes turned to Dennett. "You didn't know about the donation?"

"Not until today when I was on my way here and observed the spectacle in the lane." Dennett had been sitting back, drinking his tea, his gaze darting back and forth as Lady Agnes quizzed Nunn. A small smile hovered at the corners of Dennett's mouth, and I had the feeling he had been enjoying Nunn's discomfort. My opinion of Mr. Ernest Dennett—which was not very high to begin with—went down a notch.

Boggs entered and handed a slim folder to Lady Agnes. "From Mr. Nunn, my lady. He said to inform you he had to depart for Paddington."

Lady Agnes's eyebrows ascended. "Paddington?"

"A scholar arriving to see the collection, I believe."

"Oh yes," Lady Agnes said. "Dr. DeWitt. I'd forgotten. Quite a few things seem to be slipping my mind today. Boggs, the minute Mr. Nunn returns, I want to see him."

"Very good, my lady." Boggs left.

"Since the entertainment seems to be over for the moment, I'll leave you as well." Dennett put down his empty cup. "No, don't get up. I'll see myself out. You have much to do, unraveling the tangled web your uncle left behind for you." Halfway to the door, Dennett turned back. "You know my offer still stands, Lady Agnes." His gaze had an intensity to it that made me feel rather like a third wheel.

She gave him a brief smile. "And the answer is still the same."

"Ah, well. Doesn't hurt a chap to try. Good afternoon, ladies." I was surprised he'd remembered to include me in his goodbye. All his attention had been focused on Lady Agnes except for the brief moment he was forced to notice me when we were introduced.

As soon as the door closed behind Dennett, Lady Agnes said, "Mr. Dennett has been trying to buy Uncle Lawrence's collection for ages. The answer has always been no, and it will always be no. Unfortunately, he doesn't seem to understand that the answer will never change."

"I see." I wondered if Dennett's offer was completely about business. His tone had made the offer seem like it had more to do with romance than a business transaction.

Lady Agnes was already flipping through the pages in the slender folder Boggs had given her. "There's hardly anything in here—the original order for the cabinetry, some notes, and a few letters and invoices. The notes are about a meeting between Uncle Lawrence and Mr. Rathburn, but they only mention 'negotiations' without any details. They might have been talking about anything—some antiquity Uncle Lawrence was considering purchasing or even his concession."

"Concession?"

"His concession in the Valley of the Kings, the area Uncle Lawrence had permission to excavate." She looked back through the items in the folder. "That's another thing Mr. Dennett wanted from Uncle Lawrence." She closed it with a snap and stood.

"There's nothing of real significance in here." She tossed the folder onto her desk and picked up a small oval stone that was carved to look like a beetle. "Uncle Lawrence wouldn't give away a single scarab," she said, her thumb tracing over the carvings. "I still find the whole thing almost unbelievable." She dropped into the desk chair. Lapis poked her head out from under the desk, then hopped lightly into Lady Agnes's lap. She sighed and stroked the cat's back.

I refilled her teacup and brought it over to the desk. When things are difficult, one can't have too much tea. "If what Mr. Nunn says is true, then as shocking as the news is, it's also another argument against your uncle committing suicide."

"Goodness, that's true. I hadn't even thought of that." She nodded to the folder. "You have a look. Perhaps you'll see something I missed."

I took a seat in the chair across the desk and picked up the folder. "You could ring up your uncle's solicitors and ask if they've heard anything about it. If he intended to donate his collection, it would seem the lawyers would have to be involved."

"That's true." She put down the scarab and drew the telephone across the desk. Lapis had settled into a tight circle in her lap, and Lady Agnes continued to run her hand over the cat's back as she waited for the call to be connected.

As Lady Agnes explained to a secretary that she wanted to speak to the senior partner, I opened the thin folder. Lady Agnes's voice faded to a murmur as I skimmed the documents—the initial invoice for the cabinetry, and some notes about Lord Mulvern's meeting with Rathburn, which amounted to little more than notations of the dates of two meetings and a brief line of explanation for each, *negotiation meeting* and *further discussions of details.* A couple of letters confirming appointments completed the file. It wasn't much to go on, and I felt a little sorry for Nunn if he thought this would satisfy Lady Agnes.

A movement from Lady Agnes brought me back to the present. "I see . . . If that's the case, then I suppose there's no question." Her voice was dejected. The answer hadn't been the one she was hoping for.

"Oh!" I picked up a pencil from the desk and scribbled on the blotter. *Ask about the bequest to Hodges. When was it arranged?*

Lady Agnes frowned, but she read off my question. Her eyebrows shot straight up as she listened to the answer. "Really? And what were the details . . . ? No, no other questions. Thank you and good day." She replaced the earpiece. "Uncle Lawrence had asked the solicitors to begin drawing up paperwork to make the transfer to the museum." She tapped the note I'd written. "And Uncle Lawrence did begin arrangements for the bequest for Hodges in June of this year. It had one stipulation—that Hodges keep it absolutely confidential."

"That confirms what Hodges told me, which means Hodges didn't have much of a motive to do away with your uncle. If he was to receive the bequest in January, why would Hodges take the risk of killing your uncle a few months earlier? Unless there were some reason he needed the money immediately?"

"I think if that were the case, he would just go to my

uncle and ask for the date to be changed. Uncle Lawrence was a reasonable man. I imagine he'd have agreed—of course, I might be completely wrong. I thought I knew my uncle very well, but it appears he had a penchant for confidentiality that I wasn't aware of."

CHAPTER SIXTEEN

I twisted the bottles on the dressing table in front of me. "Oh, I wanted to wear my lily of the valley scent tonight, but I forgot to bring it. Do any of the other ladies wear it?"

Martha removed a hairpin from her mouth and slid it into my hair so that it swept my dark hair back, exposing pearl stud earrings, which matched the long string of pearls that had been my mother's. "No, miss. Lady Mulvern did wear it, but . . . um . . ." Pink crept into her cheeks. "She doesn't anymore."

It seemed Martha was the clumsy maid who'd broken Nora's bottle of scent. I had no complaints about Martha's abilities, but I imagined Nora might be a more difficult person to attend to.

I handed her another hairpin. "I heard that Nora and Gilbert had a whirlwind romance," I said, fishing for information.

Martha focused on coaxing my hair into a smooth

curve along my jawline as she murmured, "That's how it started."

"I don't know them well, but they don't seem like happy newlyweds . . ."

Even though we were alone in my room, Martha glanced side to side before she said, "They're not. They used to row constantly. Like cats and dogs, they were—each one getting the back up of the other. That's when they were engaged and first married, but now"—she shook her head—"it's just the opposite. Downright frosty with each other. There's no need for a cold room to store the fresh meat and fish if those two are around. Lord Mulvern used to be so easy-going, but he's vexed all the time now. And Lady Mulvern is scared."

"Are you sure?" Confident, sulky Nora, frightened?

Martha had dropped any pretense of arranging my hair. The hairbrush was motionless in her hands. "Oh yes, miss. In the evening Lady Mulvern always leaves the drawing room first. She comes up before Lord Mulvern and rings for Carol right away. Then after she's changed out of her evening gown, she makes Carol stay in her room until she's ready for bed, then she has Carol check the lock on the dressing room door." Martha's eyebrows expressed the significance of that detail.

So not only were Nora and Gilbert sleeping in separate rooms, Nora was locking Gilbert out. Martha added, "Lady Mulvern doesn't like to be alone. She always calls for a maid to sit with her if everyone is out. Or if she's leaving the house, she makes sure her friend Miss Gill is with her. Lady Mulvern is frightened. The scullery maids think it's because of the curse."

"What do you think?"

"It's not a phantom that's scared her, not Lady Mulvern. She's too push—" Martha seemed to suddenly remember I wasn't another maid she was gossiping with and quickly returned the brush to the dressing table. She smoothed her apron. "Will that be all, miss?"

"Yes, thank you, Martha." I stood and moved away from the dressing table. I didn't want her to worry that I'd complain about her gossiping with me, so I said, "You're brilliant at arranging hair."

She looked surprised. I supposed Nora hadn't been one to compliment her. Martha grinned. "Thank you, miss."

"Shall I make another cocktail for anyone while we wait?" Gilbert asked. We were gathered in the drawing room before dinner, and Nunn hadn't joined us yet.

"No," Nora said with a definite chilliness in her voice, which told me that the newlyweds were still not happy with each other. "I don't think we should wait any longer for Mr. Nunn. He must have taken that professor to a pub. We probably won't see either of them until tomorrow morning." Nora stood, and the intricate beading on her red dress shimmered as she moved. While the front of the dress was demure, the neckline at the back dipped almost to her waist, and a knotted string of pearls hung down between her pale shoulder blades. I was surprised she wasn't covered in goose bumps because the evening had turned chilly.

Dreary gray clouds had rolled in late in the day, and the temperature had plummeted. Tendrils of fog crept along the ground, curling around the lampposts and edges of the buildings, bringing a damp chill to the air. I'd worn my emerald-green velvet that had long sleeves and a deep ruffle down one side of the skirt in an apple-green silk. A fire crackled in the grate and the room was warm, but if I was wearing an almost backless frock, I'd have brought down a shawl.

"It's odd that he hasn't contacted us," Lady Agnes said. "I know Professor DeWitt was interested in seeing the pottery. I can't imagine he'd be put off from that."

"It's obvious, isn't it? Mr. Nunn doesn't want to face you two, even with the shielding presence of a visitor," Nora said.

Gilbert drained his cocktail. Nora had again refused his offer to make her one. "He should have informed us of Uncle Lawrence's plans."

Nora sighed. "Antiquities again. Why does everything in this family have to be about antiquities?"

"I say, that's rather unfair." Gilbert plucked his raspberry out of his drink. "Uncle Lawrence acquired a world-famous collection. Speaking of the collection"—he turned to Lady Agnes—"I hear Dennett came by today."

Lady Agnes, who had been staring into the fire, turned her head. "We were to go to the National Gallery, but I had to put it off."

Gilbert put down his empty glass. "Still after you, is he?"

"He's not after me. He's after the collection."

Nora looked to me. "Ernest Dennett lusts after

everything in the grand gallery, and he practically salivates at the mention of Uncle Lawrence's concession." She turned back to Lady Agnes. "And he knows the only way to get his hands on the antiquities or to dig in the Valley of the Kings is to marry you, Aggie."

"He'll not get it that way. He knows I have no interest in marrying him."

"Why can't Mr. Dennett dig in the Valley of the Kings?" I asked. "Surely he could get a concession as well."

"Mr. Dennett isn't on the best of terms with Pierre Dupin, who controls the concessions," Lady Agnes said.

Gilbert said, "I do believe Dennett would give up his inheritance if he could trade his site outside Cairo for one in the Valley of the Kings. He thinks Uncle Lawrence would have uncovered a new tomb if only he'd dug where Dennett told him."

"But the pyramids are near Cairo," I said. "Isn't that a good place to excavate?"

"The treasure seekers stripped the pyramids clean long ago," Lady Agnes said. "In any case, Dennett's concession isn't near the pyramids. For the last three seasons, he's dug in a small graveyard in the desert—a village graveyard—which is far beneath his aspirations. Dennett wants to discover another Tutankhamen, and the royal tombs are in the Valley of the Kings."

Nora adjusted her pearl necklace. "You're too picky, Aggie. Mr. Dennett's attractive, and he has pots of money now that his ancient uncle finally kicked off. And he actually *likes* the dusty old Egyptian stuff you adore. It would be a match made in heaven."

"She does have a point, Aggie," Gilbert said.

"I'm not marrying him."

"Give me one good reason—not an excuse, a good reason," Nora said.

"Lapis doesn't like him," she said with a grin, lightening the atmosphere.

"You're right. She always disappears when he arrives." Nora twisted around to look at the clock on the mantle. "Where is Mr. Nunn? He should have been down long ago. I know he's timid, but I didn't think he was so spineless that he'd avoid dinner."

"He has a lot to answer for," Gilbert said.

"I don't see why you're both so upset," Nora said. "It's not as if Uncle Lawrence's donation was actually arranged. Nothing's changed."

Boggs entered, and I expected him to announce dinner, but he went to Gilbert and murmured in his ear.

"The inspector?" Gilbert asked. "At this time of day?"

"How rude to arrive at dinner," Nora said. "You'd think Inspector Thorn could at least wait until tomorrow to call."

Boggs said, "It's an Inspector Longly."

Had I heard Boggs correctly? Had he said Inspector *Longly*?

"He says it's urgent information, and he must speak with you immediately," Boggs said.

Lady Agnes stepped forward. "Then show him in. He must have the results on the fingerprint analysis. Perhaps Inspector Thorn is away at the moment and this Inspector Longly is his replacement."

Boggs returned and announced Inspector Longly, who strode into the room, bringing the scent of moisture with him. He had light brown hair and a thin mustache, and his empty right-hand sleeve was pinned against his jacket as usual. He crossed the room to Gilbert. "Good evening, Lord Mulvern. I'm sorry to interrupt, but if I could speak to you in private . . ."

"That won't be necessary." Lady Agnes stepped forward. "I'm Lady Agnes, Gilbert's sister, and we're all curious about the results from the fingerprinting."

"Fingerprints? I'm not here about fingerprints."

I stood and moved to the group gathered around the inspector.

He saw me and said, "Miss Belgrave. In the thick of it again, I see."

"Good evening, Inspector Longly."

Nora glanced between the two of us. "Are you two acquainted?"

"We've met, yes." Longly said, cutting off that line of inquiry. He turned back to Gilbert. "This is the residence of Gregory Wilfred Nunn?"

"Wilfred—he goes by Wilfred Nunn," Lady Agnes said before Gilbert could answer. "Yes, he's our collection manager."

"I'm afraid I have some bad news. Mr. Nunn was killed this afternoon in a traffic accident."

"Killed?" Lady Agnes said. "Mr. Nunn? Are you sure?"

"I'm afraid there is no doubt."

"What happened?" I asked.

"He stepped in front of a lorry on Edgware Road."

"How terrible," Lady Agnes said.

Longly's gaze darted around the group, taking in each person's response to the news.

"We questioned the other pedestrians. It was quite a crush. Everyone was on the pavement, waiting for a break in traffic, when Mr. Nunn suddenly stepped into the street."

"Suddenly?" I asked.

"Yes. Several witnesses use that description." Longly removed a notebook from his pocket. "I need the direction of his family. I'll also need to examine his personal effects and to record the location of each of you today at between five and six o'clock. Purely a formality, of course."

CHAPTER SEVENTEEN

"*A*nd where were you between five and six o'clock, Miss Belgrave?" Longly asked.

"I was here at Mulvern House." I sat across the desk from Longly in what had been Nunn's office. Longly made a note of my statement, and I couldn't help but think of Nunn sitting behind the same desk only hours earlier with his ledger and pages of columns and checkmarks. Longly had summoned a constable, who sat in a corner of the room taking notes, but Longly was also jotting down his own notes with his left hand.

While Longly had examined Nunn's room and office, the rest of us had gone into dinner, but it had been an awkward meal. Lady Agnes had invited Longly to dine with us, but he'd declined. After dinner, Longly had called us one by one to be interviewed. He had saved me for last, and I didn't know if it was so I'd be more nervous, or if he assumed I was the party with the least information because I'd been in Mulvern House such a short time.

"And when did you last see Mr. Nunn?"

"This afternoon at tea. He spoke to Lady Agnes and me, then he left to meet the professor's train. Where is the professor, by the way? Was he with Nunn?"

"No," Longly said, only partially answering my questions. "I understand Mr. Nunn departed from here abruptly."

"Yes. He went to retrieve some papers for Lady Agnes but didn't return. He sent Boggs with them instead. Boggs said it was because Mr. Nunn had to meet the professor."

Longly nodded as if this information matched up with what he'd already heard. "Mr. Nunn kept back information about the late Lord Mulvern's plans for a donation to the British Museum. I understand that all came out this afternoon?"

"It did. And Mr. Nunn was distraught. You don't think . . . I mean, it wasn't suicide, was it?"

"That's what I'm trying to determine. Apparently, you're trying to determine the same thing, but in regards to the late Lord Mulvern. Yes, Lady Agnes told me she's hired you in an attempt to have the case reopened."

"And you're going to warn me off, I suppose." I thought of the note found on Lord Mulvern's desk, the one that had been trimmed shorter than the rest of the writing paper. It was currently folded into a neat bundle and tucked away in my handbag along with all the notes I'd been jotting down. I hadn't felt comfortable leaving Lord Mulvern's note in the writing desk in my room.

"If there's foul play involved, it needs to be brought

to light. However, the case was investigated, and it's been closed. I doubt you'll find your time will be productive."

No, I definitely wasn't handing over Lord Mulvern's supposed suicide note to Longly—not yet. It would take more than an unusual size of paper to convince him there was more to Lord Mulvern's death than suicide. "You're saying Inspector Thorn pursued all possibilities around Lord Mulvern's death? Because Inspector Thorn certainly wasn't meticulous when he came to investigate the break-in yesterday."

"A break-in is in a very different category than a death," Longly said. "Besides, when the verdict of an inquest is suicide, the investigation ends. Thorn would have been foolish to spend his time continuing to dig into the details. We have plenty of other criminal cases to investigate."

So Longly wasn't going to warn me off, but only because he felt there was nothing to find. "So, in your opinion, it's a wild goose chase?"

"Perhaps," he said mildly. "In regard to the break-in, the fingerprint report has just come in." He turned back the page in his notebook and read from it. "One clear set of prints belonging to Mr. Wilfred Nunn, found on the interior of the glass case. No other discernible prints."

"Well, that's not conclusive," I said. "Mr. Nunn was the collection manager. I'm sure his fingerprints are on everything in the grand gallery. He was most distraught when he saw the damage to the mummy."

"Was he?" Longly picked up an envelope. "Perhaps he had a touch of the theatrical about him." Longly tipped out the contents of the envelope. Several smooth, brightly colored oval stones clattered onto the desktop along with a necklace and some rings.

I recognized the oval stones. "Those are scarabs." They were similar to the ones I'd seen on Lady Agnes's desk, but one was much larger. I reached out, but Longly held up a warning hand. "Please don't touch. Fingerprints, you know. They haven't been tested yet." He nudged one of the stones with the envelope. "Lady Agnes tells me these are authentic Egyptian scarabs, likely from the damaged mummy."

"She can tell they came from the mummy?"

"Apparently, the large dark gray one has a name carved into the flat surface that identifies the person it was made for— the heart scarab, Lady Agnes called it. She said it would have been put into the mummy over the man's heart and buried with him." Longly waved the envelope over the scarabs and jewelry. "I found these hidden under Mr. Nunn's mattress."

"Mr. Nunn's? You think Mr. Nunn cut open the mummy and took these?" I sat back in the chair, my thoughts racing.

"You seem to think that's a far-fetched idea?"

"Only because Mr. Nunn didn't seem the type of person who would damage a mummy—especially the Zozar mummy," I said, thinking of the way he'd spoken the mummy's name when he'd arrived in the gallery. Had his emotion been an act, a clever feint?

"But he was passionate about antiquities," Longly said. "And Mr. Nunn thought the mummy should be unwrapped, which I understand Lady Agnes refused to do."

"Then that would mean Mr. Nunn staged the broken window in the scullery and the muddy footprints. It was all a ruse to make us think it was an outsider."

"Yes." Longly said the word with no surprise or amazement in his tone.

Nunn was small enough that he would be able to fit through the window. "If that's the case, Thorn was correct when he said it was an inside job."

"While Thorn does not have the best . . . *bedside manner*, shall we say, he's a canny old chap." Longly closed his notebook, then used a pencil to push the scarabs back into the envelope, which he tucked away in his jacket. "Thank you for your time, Miss Belgrave. That will be all."

When I returned to the drawing room, Nora was saying, ". . . timid little Mr. Nunn? He stumped up enough courage to damage the mummy and steal some tiny Egyptian trinkets, then threw himself in front of the lorry because he regretted not telling us about some silly donation to a museum?"

"It wasn't a silly little donation," Lady Agnes said. "It was Uncle Lawrence's entire collection."

"All the better," Nora said. "It would have gotten these creepy old things out of the house." She swiveled on the sofa and turned to Gilbert, who was sunk deep in an arm chair near the fire. "In fact, why don't you do that, Gilbert? Then we wouldn't be burdened with all these dusty antiquities."

Before Gilbert could respond, Lady Agnes said, "Give everything away?"

Her voice trembled with emotion—anger, I realized. And it dawned on me that Nunn wasn't the only person who had a motive to prevent the late Lord Mulvern from giving away his collection. Lady Agnes was also highly invested in it. It was clear she wouldn't have welcomed the idea of donating it, which was probably why her uncle had kept his plans secret from his family.

"Now is not the time to discuss anything of that sort," Gilbert said in the firmest tone I'd ever heard him use.

Nora's lower lip protruded into a pout. She surged to her feet. "Well, I'm not going to sit around here any longer this evening. I'm going to bed—alone."

A scowl settled on Gilbert's face as he watched her cross the room.

Inspector Longly came into the room moments after Nora exited. He said he'd be in touch the next day and departed. I announced I was going up to my room. Neither Lady Agnes nor Gilbert protested my retiring early, and I suspected they wanted to have a chat by themselves.

I felt very much the outsider as I climbed the stairs. I'd thought I was working with Lady Agnes, that we were allies striving for the same goal—the truth about her uncle's death. But I'd seen a side of her tonight that I hadn't expected. She dearly loved the Egyptian antiquities and would not have been happy to see them transferred to the British Museum. She hadn't known about the donation until that day—had she? Was she acting outraged to cover up prior knowledge? But then, why would she hire me? I'd thought she sincerely wanted the truth. Had I been wrong? I rubbed my temple and rang for Martha.

Once I was in my dressing gown and Martha had departed, I sank down at the writing desk and noted everything that had happened that day. My hand was quite cramped by the time I finished, and I didn't have any clarity on what was happening at Mulvern House. Everything seemed to be even more of a muddle than when I arrived.

CHAPTER EIGHTEEN

When I came down the stairs the next morning, Boggs was standing at a gilded chest of drawers in the entrance hall, near the foot of the stairs. The entry didn't get the morning sun, and Boggs's dark-suited form was barely distinguishable in the dim light. Only his pale hands flashed as he sorted the light-colored envelopes. "Good morning, Boggs," I said as I stepped off the stairs' red runner. Boggs's shoulders twitched, and I said, "I'm sorry. I didn't mean to startle you."

"Not at all, miss." Boggs held out a salver. "Some letters arrived for you in the morning post."

I recognized Essie's hurried script on one, and the other had Jasper's neat penmanship. I read them on my way to the breakfast room. The first, from Essie, instructed me to meet her that morning at Lyons. Normally, I would have bristled at a summons, but she must have news, which didn't surprise me at all. Once

Essie set her mind to something, there was no stopping her.

Jasper's note was short as well.

In town for a few days and have greetings to pass on to you from your cousins and your aunt. Would you like to meet later this morning? Because you have such an excessive interest in exercise, I intended to ask if you'd like to stroll in the park, but that would be less than enjoyable—and possibly dangerous—in the dense fog. However, I do have a hankering to stroll around the National Gallery and will be there today from 11 o'clock on, if you'd care to join me.

So Jasper was back. He had a tendency to disappear without explanation then reappear, rather like a genie popping out of a lamp. Despite his tendency to travel unpredictably, I knew he'd keep his word and be in the National Gallery today. I'd meet him there after I talked with Essie.

I put the letters in my pocket as I entered the breakfast room. Lady Agnes was already at the table. I said good morning and went to fill my plate. As I returned from the sideboard, Boggs entered. "The post has arrived, my lady."

Lady Agnes took the single letter from the salver Boggs offered and went completely still.

I put my plate down on the table. "Are you all right, Lady Agnes?"

"It's from Mr. Nunn." Lady Agnes examined the envelope a moment. "It must've been posted yesterday evening. Before . . ." She hesitated a moment, then opened the envelope and took out a sheet of paper. She skimmed the note, and the color drained from her face, leaving her complexion as white as the linen tablecloth. She pressed her hand to her mouth. "Oh my."

"What is it?" I asked.

"It's terrible, but it also contains an answer . . ." She skimmed the paper again, then she recovered some of her usual authoritative manner. "Boggs, telephone Inspector Longly. Tell him he must come here at once."

"Very good, my lady." Boggs left the room.

Lady Agnes handed the letter to me. "It's a confession. Mr. Nunn says he poisoned my uncle to prevent the donation of the collection, but he couldn't stand the guilt. It—it's a suicide note."

CHAPTER NINETEEN

I left my room after breakfast, my thoughts spinning like a top I'd played with as a child, darting in one direction then wobbling off in another. Nunn, a murderer? He hadn't figured prominently in my suspicions until I learned about the donation, but his knowledge of the donation did give him a motive. Like everyone in the house that night, he had opportunity.

But that letter . . . something about it was a bit off. Was it the tone? The word choice?

The letter itself was short enough that I could remember it almost word for word.

The guilt is unbearable. I confess to taking Lord Mulvern's life. There, I've put it down. Now there is no other choice but to end it all. I'm sorry.

Wilfred Nunn.

I was halfway down the stairs and in the process of pulling on my gloves when I stopped short. The signature! That was what bothered me. I checked my wristwatch. I was supposed to meet Essie in a quarter of an hour, but I had time for a short detour.

The morning room was empty, and I hurried to Lady Agnes's desk. I wanted to complete my task and leave as quickly as possible. If anyone found me riffling through the papers on her desk, it would be quite awkward. I was sure the letter I'd watched Nunn sign the day before was gone—probably dispatched in the post—but the folder of correspondence Nunn had brought for Lady Agnes to look over had contained several letters and forms with his signature. I'd left it on her desk, and I was relieved to see it was still there.

I hooked my handbag's short strap over my wrist as I picked up the folder and paged through it. I'd been focused on the content of the letters and forms before, but now I was only interested in the signatures. My gaze tracked to the bottom of each page as I flicked through them. Nunn had signed each piece of correspondence exactly the way I'd seen him sign the letter, *G. Wilfred Nunn*.

I repositioned the folder on the desk and headed for the door, but before I reached it, I heard voices. Lady Agnes's voice drifted down the hall. "... quite shocking to open a letter from Mr. Nunn this morning."

"Yes, I imagine so," Longly said.

Lady Agnes's voice became more distinct as she drew closer. "I locked it in my desk drawer."

My heartbeat jumped. They were coming in here. I didn't want to become entangled in answering more questions from Longly. I darted behind the open door, snuggling into the triangle of space between the door and the wall.

"I can't figure out what happened to Professor DeWitt." I caught a glimpse of Lady Agnes's black curls and Longly's dark suit as they passed through the doorway. "He should have arrived last evening," Lady Agnes said. "In all the confusion, I completely forgot about him until now."

"He never left Oxford," Longly said as they crossed the room. "He fell ill two days ago and wrote a letter informing you he had to delay his trip. Unfortunately, he put the wrong house number on the letter, and it was delivered across the square. I've just come from speaking to Mr. Clark."

"It went to Mr. Clark? Goodness. No wonder we didn't know about it. Mr. Clark spends days on end at his club. He probably never even saw it."

"I called on him at his club, and he gave me permission to look for the letter. It was in a stack of mail waiting for his attention. It hadn't even been opened yet."

The jingle of metal sounded. Lady Agnes must be taking out a set of keys to unlock the drawer. "Then Mr. Nunn would have waited at the train station, and when he realized the professor wasn't arriving, he must have left. Here's the letter."

I poked my head around the door. Lady Agnes and Longly stood with their backs to me.

Now was the time to slip out. As Longly slid the paper out of the envelope and unfolded it, I took three careful steps on my tiptoes, then dodged out the door.

"I'd like to see some of Mr. Nunn's correspondence . . ." Longly's voice faded as I scurried down the passageway, grateful for the carpet runner that muffled my steps. Thank goodness I already had on my hat and gloves and could slip out of Mulvern House straight-away. Within a minute, I plunged out the front door and into the fog.

Once I'd left the circular drive of Mulvern House, I paced along, keeping close to the buildings as I peered ahead, looking for the next lamppost, which emerged out of the fog as I neared it. It wouldn't do to drift off the pavement into the road. Traffic was light, but the rumble of an engine signaled the approach of a motor every few minutes, then the yellow beams of their headlights cut through the white haze only yards away. I used the fuzzy glowing chain of the streetlights to navigate through the fog. A few other pedestrians were out as well. For those who were coming in my direction, I could hear the click of their heels long before they materialized in my little bubble of visibility for a moment, then the fog swallowed them up again.

I adjusted the lapels of my coat higher over my throat against the chill. Would Longly pick up on the missing initial on the signature of the letter Lady Agnes had received that morning? It was a small thing, the absence of a first initial, but on all the other papers I'd looked at, Nunn had always signed with the initial *G* before the rest of his name. It was hard to believe he'd suddenly change his signature at the last moment.

If the signature was wrong on the note, then Nunn didn't write it, which meant the odds were high that he didn't step in front of that lorry intentionally. This brought up another long list of questions. Who would do that to Nunn? Who *could* have done that to Nunn? Did someone slip out of Mulvern House the previous evening and follow Nunn? When the professor didn't arrive, did someone realize it was a chance to do away with Nunn and place the blame for Lord Mulvern's death on him?

I'd have to be careful not to betray the news of Nunn's death to Essie. If she thought there was even a hint of a juicy bit of news, she'd keep at me until she got it out of me. It was better not to think about it right now. It was too soon to tell her what had happened. Too many questions were unanswered, and I didn't even know if Nunn's family had been informed.

I was glad to see the lights of the Lyons Corner House shining through the mist. I found Essie upstairs, seated at a table by the window. She wore another cloche hat, this one covered in ruched silk shaped into flowers along with several feathers that dipped down and almost covered her eyes.

"Good morning, Essie."

She had been hunched over a small notebook, but she snapped it closed. "Olive, I'm glad you could meet me. Such exciting news—"

I put my handbag on the table as I settled into my chair.

"Goodness, Olive. Careful where you point that."

"What? Oh—" The clasp of my purse had unfastened, and the mouth of the bag had fallen open. The shiny metallic compact that was shaped like a gun sparkled in the lights of the restaurant. Essie poked at my handbag, turning it so that the muzzle of the "gun" faced me, not her.

"It's not real," I said. "It's a compact." I angled the purse a little bit and shifted the compact around so Essie could see the thin line where the two halves of the metal met.

"How clever. I need one of those. Where did you get it?"

"It was a gift." I closed my handbag and scooted my chair closer to the table. "You found the source, didn't you?"

"Yes." Satisfaction infused her tone.

I didn't doubt for a moment that she would be able to find out. "Who is it?"

Essie opened her mouth, but then the nippy arrived. We both ordered pots of tea and buttered toast.

"Well?" I thought Essie might try to drag the suspense out, but she leaned over the table and lowered her voice, even though the restaurant hummed with conversation and the clatter of cutlery. "Lady Mulvern."

I straightened. "Nora?"

"Yes. Narcissistic Nora herself," Essie said with a nod.

I looked out the window. The fog blurred the building across the street into a hazy impressionistic outline. "But that doesn't make sense."

"It doesn't sound at all like Nora, I grant you that, but once I got a little liquor into Charlie, he told all.

Except for the original story about the suicide note that ran right after Lord Mulvern's death, everything else has been from Nora."

"But not the first story that was published?"

"No. That was a tip from the police."

"Interesting." That was a tangent, and I needed to stay focused. "Regardless of the first story, why would Nora give the reporter—how many others? Four, five?"

"Five." Essie tapped the table in front of me. "That's what I'm counting on you to find out. There has to be a reason."

"The only reason that I can think of for Nora to give information to a reporter would be to see her picture in the paper, but none of the articles mentioned her or ran her picture." What game was Nora playing? Why was she planting articles in the newspapers to drag the family into the news? Did she think that somehow that ploy would get her the flat she wanted? Perhaps she thought if Mulvern House had a reputation for being a spooky, unsavory sort of place, Gilbert would want to move?

The waitress arrived with our order, which brought my attention back to the table.

Essie picked up her toast. "I hear you're staying at Mulvern House."

Of course Essie had picked up that nugget of information as well. "Lady Agnes asked me to stay for a few days."

"Intriguing, considering you and Lady Agnes aren't close friends."

"Lady Agnes and I are recent acquaintances," I hedged.

"It would seem that if anyone were going to issue you an invitation to stay at Mulvern House, it would be Nora. After all, you and I both knew her at finishing school."

I gave Essie a quick smile. "I promise I'll tell you all the details when the situation is sorted out."

She sighed, reaching for another piece of toast. "I knew you'd say that. I won't push for details now because you've been good enough to contact me in the past with some choice news stories."

"I'm doing my best to give your career a boost. Us working girls do have to stick together."

"And I need all the help I can get—especially with Charlie hoovering up all the sensational stories." She stared out the window a moment. "I don't see how he does it, considering how lazy he is. He barely gets his stories typed up before deadline. Where he finds the energy to track down news, I don't know."

We spent the rest of our time together with Essie sharing all the social gossip she knew. We parted in the fog outside the restaurant. Essie twined a scarf around her neck and gave an exaggerated shiver. "Dreadful weather. What I wouldn't give for a glimpse of the Mediterranean." She lifted her arm and hailed a taxi. "The ladies' meeting I'm covering next is only a few blocks away, but this weather is too nasty to endure." She paused with her hand on the handle of the taxi door. "Do let me know what you find out. I can't wait to trump old Charlie."

CHAPTER TWENTY

*T*endrils of fog swirled around me as I set off. The National Gallery wasn't that far away, and I couldn't quite justify the extravagance of a taxi. The habit of thriftiness had become ingrained in me, and while I knew I had money in the bank and Lady Agnes had provided a nice retainer, I couldn't bring myself to indulge in such a frivolous thing as a taxi ride for a short distance.

I found Jasper leaning on his walking stick in front of a painting in shades of black and gray that looked as if someone had painted a scene then taken a rag and wiped it round the canvas, blurring the image.

I stopped a little behind his shoulder. "That one's terribly grim. Perhaps we could find something a little cheerier."

Jasper turned, and his eyes crinkled as he smiled. "Hello, old thing. I'm glad you came. I thought you might stay in because of the fog."

"If I let the weather dictate my actions, I might never leave home. This is London, after all."

"The motto of a true Londoner." He angled his stick at the painting. "I thought it fit with the atmosphere of the day."

"It fits with my current state of mind."

"And what would that be?"

"A muddle."

"Sounds fascinating." He extended his arm. "You can tell me all about it while we stroll in search of something brighter."

"And more . . . recognizable. A nice, undemanding landscape would be ideal." I linked my arm through his. "Before I launch into my story, I must hear what you've been doing, where you've been. You said you had a message from Aunt Caroline, Gwen, and Violet?"

"Your relatives send their love and wish me to inform you that they will return before the month is out."

"And did you see them in the South of France?" I asked as we moved at a stately pace through the galleries, pausing occasionally in front of paintings.

"No, I ran across them while strolling in the Tuileries Garden. It was the first chance they had had to see the city. Apparently, the rest of their time had been spent at the *modiste*."

"I would laugh, but I know that's not a joke. Aunt Caroline takes her fashion very seriously."

"Perhaps this one?" Jasper tilted his head at a painting of a bright field of wildflowers and an expansive sky.

"Yes. It's exactly what I need today. Something clear and beautiful to help me think."

"And a sounding board?" Jasper asked.

"You know you're much more to me than just a sounding board." I cleared my throat. I was incredibly fond of Jasper—and I thought he felt the same about me—but it was one of those things we didn't mention, and I didn't let myself think about it too much. I hurried on. "As I said, things are in quite a muddle at Mulvern House."

"How so?"

"Lady Agnes thinks her uncle didn't commit suicide. She believes he was murdered."

"And she asked you to help her . . . prove that?"

"She hired me, yes."

"And have you made any progress on this endeavor?"

"Of a sort. I've uncovered several things that have been going on within Mulvern House, but nothing definite. I'll start at the beginning. The late Lord Mulvern died of an overdose of sleeping powders, which he did take occasionally, but the dose that ended his life was considerably more than any person would pour into their glass."

"So, not an accident, then."

"Definitely not. The inquest verdict was suicide. As far as I've been able to determine, everyone in the household that evening had an opportunity to slip into Lord Mulvern's room and add the Veronal to the tumbler of water that was kept beside his bed. Lord Mulvern hosted a dinner party the night before he died. The family was there along with Mr. Rathburn."

Jasper lifted an eyebrow. "Good heavens. Albert Rathburn, a suspect?"

"He has to be on the list. He was there."

"I'm sure he didn't take that well."

"He seemed to have a sudden case of amnesia regarding any details around the dinner party."

"In one way, you're fortunate. It's probably the only time Rathburn hasn't been verbose."

"So you do know him well."

"I've dined with him a few times."

"Yes, well, he only spoke to me because Lady Agnes insisted. But I'm getting ahead of myself. To go back to the beginning—Nora, you remember her? Nora Clayton before she married Gilbert?"

At Jasper's nod, I said, "She was quite sure Lord Mulvern's valet, Hodges, had added the extra Veronal because Hodges received a hefty legacy on Lord Mulvern's death. However, I don't think he did it. He was to receive the same legacy when he left service at Mulvern House, which he'd arranged to do in a few months. Hodges would be taking a great—and unnecessary —risk if he were to murder Lord Mulvern."

Jasper motioned to a bench across the room. "It was a large bequest?"

"Large enough to purchase a flat in Belgravia."

"Dashed generous of Mulvern."

"Hodges served with him in the war."

"Ah. I see."

As we settled on the bench, I said, "Except for the butler, Boggs, the rest of the servants have been with the family for practically eons, and there were no other stipulations for large legacies to any of them, so I don't see how any of them could have benefited from Lord Mulvern's death. I can't quite sort out Boggs. It appears he's related to an antiques dealer."

"There's no law against that."

"No, but there was a break-in at Mulvern House, and some antiquities were stolen—although that may be resolved," I said, thinking of scarabs Longly had found in Nunn's room, which was awfully convenient. "Or possibly not. Getting back to the suspects, Gilbert doesn't want me there, and he doesn't want to talk about the evening of his uncle's death."

"Perhaps he's still grieving."

"Perhaps. He doesn't want to discuss it at all. While he shut down any inquiry from me, I've discovered Nora, on the other hand, has been feeding details to the newspapers for their stories about the mummy's curse."

Jasper's gaze had drifted to a nearby portrait, but he swiveled toward me. "How bizarre."

"Isn't it? And lastly, their collection manager committed suicide—supposedly—last night. He stepped in front of a lorry, but before that, he sent a note confessing to murdering Lord Mulvern."

Jasper looked at me for a long moment. "He sent a note around?"

"Yes. He used the Royal Mail to deliver his suicide note, which is only one part of the incident that seems odd to me. If Mr. Nunn did murder Lord Mulvern, then Mr. Nunn's death ties everything up in a neat little package."

"But if he didn't do it, then it lets a murderer go free. Yes, I see your concern."

"The problem with this sort of situation is that there

are no clues left, no evidence to prove Mr. Nunn didn't pour that mixture of sleeping powders—or that anyone else did. As I said to Lady Agnes, it's very difficult to disprove something."

"That is a rub."

"I saw the note from Mr. Nunn. There was something a bit queer about it. It took me a while to work it out, but then I realized what it was."

I explained about the difference in signatures, and Jasper asked, "Do you think Inspector Longly will pick up on it?"

"I believe so. When I left Mulvern House this morning, Inspector Longly had asked to see Mr. Nunn's correspondence. I'm sure if I picked up on it, Inspector Longly will as well." I didn't mention I'd been snooping around Lady Agnes's desk. Jasper tended to get a little fussy about some of my activities.

"Speaking of notes," I said, "I left out another note— you can see how jumbled my mind is because I forgot to tell you about this one. Lady Agnes gave me the note found on her uncle's desk the morning he died."

One of Jasper's eyebrows arched. "She gave it to you?"

"She wanted me to have all the information related to her uncle's death." I took it out of my handbag and gave it to him. It was still enclosed in the larger sheet of plain writing paper that I'd taken from the desk.

Both of Jasper's eyebrows went up. "You're carrying it around with you?"

"Yes. It could be a valuable clue." I pointed out the snipped-off portion at the top.

Jasper took out his monocle. "I knew this would

come in handy someday," he said as he put it to his eye then studied the edge of the paper. He removed the monocle. "Olive, old girl, you're the bee's knees. You're right. It definitely looks as if it's been tampered with." His expression shifted to a frown. "You should have given it to Longly straightaway."

"But Longly wasn't on the case then—and there's no case. It was closed, remember? And perhaps Lord Mulvern trimmed off the top of the page himself. Or he simply picked up a piece of paper that had been cut for some other purpose—that's what the police would say. It's not evidence he didn't commit suicide, just that he didn't use a full sheet of paper to write his note."

"All the same, I think at this point you'd be wise to hand this over to Longly."

"I considered doing that very thing yesterday, but then Inspector Longly practically told me I wouldn't find anything amiss about Lord Mulvern's death."

Jasper put his monocle away. "All the same, the police should have it."

I sighed. "I suppose you're right. Things have changed, especially now that it looks as if Mr. Nunn might have been murdered. There are just so many loose ends I would like to tie up."

"You'd like to present the inspector a nice little package with a bow on top?"

I shifted on the bench. "I suppose that's my pride showing, but it's true. Lady Agnes asked me to look into this. I've worked hard to search out what really happened. I want to see how it turns out."

"And you want to be the one to figure it out."

"Wouldn't you?"

Jasper waved a hand. "No. Much too exhausting, all that cogitation."

"It's not all cogitation. Most of it is just good old-fashioned legwork and asking questions."

"How so?"

"Well, take Boggs. I followed him to the antiques shop. That was simply noticing he looked as if he wanted to make sure he wasn't followed, which meant he was going somewhere he didn't want anyone to know about." I sighed again. "There's something going on with him. I haven't quite figured out what it is."

"Because of his relative?"

"Don't you think it's a little too coincidental that his relative owns an antiques shop and antiquities have been stolen from Mulvern House?"

"It could be a coincidence." Jasper's tone had a trace of doubt in it as he stared across the gallery, his gaze unfocused. He handed the note to me. "Well, I don't see why you can't hand this off to the good inspector and continue your discreet inquiries. In fact, why don't you deliver that note to Inspector Longly while I toddle off and visit this establishment of Boggs's relative? You've already been there once, and I daresay he'd remember a young woman of your breeding. I won't draw nearly as much attention."

"And you'd be unmemorable?" I ran my gaze over him from his golden hair to his immaculate and obviously expensive suit. "You don't think he'd remember such a dapper gentleman as yourself?"

"I wouldn't go in this. I'll change into a suit from last year."

"Oh, that will make you nearly invisible, I'm sure."

"Don't scoff. Fortunately, it's Grigsby's afternoon off. Otherwise he'd block the door if he saw me leaving my rooms in outdated attire."

"And are you in the habit of visiting antique shops in rather questionable parts of town?"

"A true collector is never particular about where the search takes him. Perhaps this establishment stocks books. I'm looking for a volume of crime fiction that escaped me when it first came out . . ."

"Just don't forget what you're actually after—information about Boggs, the butler, or anything related to the theft of antiquities at Mulvern House."

"I always discharge my duties." Jasper reached for his walking stick.

I put the note in my handbag, and we stood. "I do appreciate you going on my behalf. I hope it doesn't intrude on your schedule."

"I have nothing pressing on my schedule until Friday when I leave town," Jasper said as we strolled out of the gallery.

"You're leaving again so soon? You just returned."

"One must honor one's social commitments. I find hostesses become quite testy when one reneges on an invitation."

"Where are you off to?"

"A shooting party in Scotland."

"I didn't know you had taken up hunting." In all the years I'd known Jasper, he'd never shown much interest in the sport.

"Not my line, but there are so few men now who can handle the sound of the gunshots. My hostess was quite desperate and sent an invitation around to me."

"I doubt desperation was involved. You're considered quite a catch."

"Yes, I know—I have all my own hair and teeth."

"That's not what I meant, but I do agree those things are a step up from several eligible bachelors I've been paired with recently."

As we passed through the doors and stepped into the gray day, Jasper said, "A good head of hair will get a man no end of dinner invitations. I'll send a telegram if I find anything of interest."

CHAPTER TWENTY-ONE

*J*asper insisted on putting me in a taxi and paying for my fare, so I settled back against the seat and enjoyed the luxury of being driven to Mulvern House. As the taxi pulled under the porte-cochère, Longly came out of the front door. I was in the middle of another debate with myself about whether or not I should turn over the note to Longly, but I reminded myself that Nunn might have been pushed, and I swung open the taxi door. "Inspector!" I called. "Would you take a turn around the square with me? I have some information you might find useful."

"Certainly," Longly said. I could tell he'd rather not delay his departure from Mulvern House, but he was too polite to turn me down.

I scooted over to the far side of the seat, and Longly slid in beside me.

"Once around the square, please," I said to the driver. "And take it slowly."

The driver seem to want to refuse, but Longly said, "Scotland Yard will pay the extra charge."

"Right you are, gov'nor."

We didn't have long, so I didn't waste time. "Lady Agnes gave me the note that was found on Lord Mulvern's desk after he died. Have you seen it?"

"Not my case, so, no."

I removed the paper from my handbag. He took it from me with the same look of surprise that had been on Jasper's face, so I said, "I've found rooms in town houses are often quite like those in country homes. It's difficult to secure items with any certainty. I felt more comfortable keeping it with me."

He inclined his head. "That is true." He opened the paper and glanced over the brief note. "And you think I need to see this now. Why?"

With a glance at the driver, I lowered my voice. "Because I think you noticed the same thing I did about the note from Mr. Nunn, that it wasn't signed with Mr. Nunn's usual signature. I think someone forged the note from Mr. Nunn and planted the scarabs so Mr. Nunn would take the blame for Lord Mulvern's murder."

The taxi jerked suddenly to the left.

"Sorry," the driver said with a long glance over his shoulder.

"Drive on," Longly said.

The driver turned back to look through the windshield, but I knew he was listening to every word we said.

"Look at the paper." I pointed to the top edge and showed him the size difference between it and the plain writing paper from the desk, which I still had. I pointed out the scissor notches and the slight slope.

Longly held the papers up to the light and narrowed his eyes as he studied the edges, then lowered his voice so much that I could barely hear him. "So someone tampered with Lord Mulvern's suicide note?"

"It does seem that way."

Longly folded the letter back into thirds with the plain sheet around it. "I'll hold onto this for now." He put it in an inside pocket. "How much longer are you staying at Mulvern House?"

"I'm not sure. Lady Agnes has asked me to stay indefinitely."

"I think you'd be better off returning to your own lodgings."

"Why?"

We'd made the complete trip around Mulvern Square. The driver slowed the taxi even more as we neared Mulvern House. "Where to?"

"Through the gates, if you please," Longly said, and the taxi pulled under the porte-cochère. Longly held the door open for me, then reached back in to pay the driver. "There's a tip in there for you. If I hear this conversation has been repeated, I'll know the source."

"No worries, gov'nor." The driver took the money and touched his brow. "Me hearing is going. Can't hardly make out anything nowadays."

The taxi pulled way, and Longly turned back to me. "If you're correct, if someone did . . . *hasten* Lord Mulvern's death—and it's a possibility we must consider with the odd signature on the note from Mr. Nunn—then someone has killed again in an effort to hide the first murder. The more you stir things up, the worse it will be. At this moment, Lady Agnes doesn't think Mr. Nunn's death was anything more than a horrible accident. It will be safer for her and for you if that remains the status quo."

"She didn't notice the difference in the signatures?"

"No. Mr. Nunn's death rattled her so much that she overlooked it. I did ask to see some of his correspondence today, but I said it was because I needed to verify his handwriting. I didn't call attention to the signature. You're much safer if you leave this alone and let us sort it out."

"Are you ordering me to leave Mulvern House?"

"Order you?" Longly laughed. "As if you'd follow any instructions of that sort. No. I know you, Miss Belgrave. Your cousin Gwen might do as I asked, but not you." He hesitated a moment, and I thought he was going to ask after Gwen, but then he went on, "If I gave that sort of command, you'd be more likely to entrench yourself more deeply. I can only give you my best advice and that would be to leave.

Good afternoon, Miss Belgrave." He tipped his hat and disappeared into the fog.

CHAPTER TWENTY-TWO

a footman opened the door for me at Mulvern House. "Where's Boggs?" I asked as I stepped inside.

"He's been called away on a family emergency. His mother was suddenly taken ill."

"I'm sorry to hear that. Where did he go?"

"Northumberland, miss."

The timing of Boggs's sudden departure seemed suspicious. Perhaps his mother was indeed ill . . . or perhaps it had more to do with the letter I'd asked Lady Agnes to write to check his references. He'd been in the hallway, so he must have overheard us discussing it. Then another thought struck me—could it be related to Nunn's death?

Before I could parse my thoughts on which was the more likely scenario, Nora came down the stairs, wearing a hat. Her gloved hand trailed along the banister, and her skirt flared as she practically ran down the stairs. "Has the inspector left?" she asked the footman.

"Yes, my lady, just a few moments ago."

What I thought was a look of relief flashed across Nora's face.

"Did you need to speak to him?" I asked.

"No, I just wanted to make sure he'd gone," Nora said, then told the footman, "I need my coat, the mink."

When the footman departed to retrieve the coat, I asked, "Nora, do you have a moment?"

She squinted at the grandfather clock on the other side of the entry. "Not really. Dorothy should be here any moment. She's going with me to Madame LaFoy's. There's just enough time to pick up my new hat before dinner."

"It's rather important."

"Oh, very well," she said. "What is it?"

I tilted my head to the stairs. "Perhaps we could go upstairs into the drawing room."

She sighed. "I suppose." She didn't exactly stomp up the stairs, but she certainly made it clear that she wasn't happy about speaking to me. When we entered the drawing room, Lapis dropped down from the windowsill and made her way lightly across the rug to twine around Nora's feet.

I checked to make sure no servants were lingering in the hall, then I closed the door. "Why have you been feeding information to the newspapers?"

Nora picked up the cat and nuzzled her chin against its head. "I don't know what you're talking about."

"Nora, now is not the time for playacting."

"But something like that is preposterous. You shouldn't listen to rumors."

"It's true. The reporter I spoke to mentioned you by name."

Nora burrowed her cheek against the cat's creamy fur for a moment, then she looked up and lifted her chin. "What if I have? There's nothing that says I can't talk to whomever I like."

"But you're intentionally spreading rumors—preposterous rumors, I might add—about a mummy's curse on this house. Why would you do that?"

"It's none of your business. I don't know why you think you can come in here and poke your nose into our business." She held Lapis curled up against her chest and stroked her hand down the cat's spine in a quick pattern. "You're not even a close family friend. I don't have to answer to you."

Lapis squirmed, and Nora released her. The cat landed lightly, then came over and sniffed my shoes. Nora brushed cat hairs off her sleeve. "I expect you to keep this to yourself."

"I can't do that. Lady Agnes hired me to find out what happened to her uncle and stop the rumors, and I intend to do that."

Nora's hand stilled. "You wouldn't tell Aggie—"

"I'm afraid you're not giving me another choice." Even though Nora and I had known each other at finishing school, she wasn't a close friend, and she'd never done anything to inspire loyalty in me. It was Lady Agnes who had hired me.

Nora must have realized from my expression that I was serious and she wouldn't be able to change my mind. She made an exasperated sound and turned away. She strode to one of the windows on the far side of the room, where she gazed out at the view of the park, which was still almost completely obscured by the fog.

"I've come to you first, Nora," I said. "I could've gone to Lady Agnes or Gilbert, but I wanted to speak to you."

"And I know how persistent you are. You won't stop, will you?"

"No." I hadn't promised Inspector Longly that I would stop asking questions, and I didn't intend to.

"Very well," she said with a sigh. "I'll tell you. I didn't know what else to do." She turned away from the window and clenched the edge of a wingback chair. "I don't know where that first story about the curse came from, but when I saw it, I realized what a good distraction it was."

"A distraction?"

"Yes. It was before the inquest. I didn't want the newspapers to focus on the family. It seemed better that all that newsprint go toward some supernatural curse, something that was completely absurd. No one would actually believe it, but everyone loved the idea of it."

"But what did you need to distract from in the first place?"

"Because I saw Gilbert leave Uncle Lawrence's room that evening."

Her voice was so low and so hesitant, I had to stain to hear her.

"But Gilbert said he didn't go into his uncle's room that night."

She shoved away from the chair and said in her normal tones, "Well, he lied. He lied to the investigators, to me, to his sister, and to you." Her voice was fierce as she went on. "I couldn't contradict him. He was my husband. And I knew if word got out he'd been in there, everyone would think Gilbert had killed Uncle Lawrence for his money."

"Which was a contentious subject between you and Gilbert as well as between you and Lord Mulvern."

"We did fight about money, Gilbert and I. We didn't want much." She waved a hand around the room. "Imagine how much this town house cost—all these furnishings, the endless antiquities. Uncle Lawrence could have easily provided a flat for Gilbert and me. He just didn't want to spend the money. If it wasn't antiquities, Uncle Lawrence wasn't interested."

She dropped onto the sofa. "I did argue with Uncle Lawrence earlier that afternoon. Our voices were quite . . . noticeable. Gilbert heard us."

"And so when you saw Gilbert go into his uncle's room, you thought . . ."

"I didn't think anything at the time. I'd actually been in his room myself only a few minutes earlier."

"You went into Lord Mulvern's room as well that evening?" It appeared Gilbert wasn't the only liar at Mulvern House.

"I only stepped in for a moment," Nora said as if the briefness of her visit meant she hadn't lied as well. "I was on my way down to dinner and found one of Uncle Lawrence's cufflinks on the floor in the hall. It was a ruby and diamond cufflink. Lapis was batting it back and forth across the rug, and the sparkle of the stones caught my attention. That's the only reason I noticed it. I couldn't leave it lying on the rug. It's quite valuable, you know. Uncle Lawrence's door was right there. The simplest thing was to walk in and drop it in the little dish on his bureau, which I did."

"Was there anyone else with you in the hallway when you found the cufflink?"

"No. I picked up the cufflink. Lapis was quite upset I interrupted her game." Nora looked across the room. Lapis ambled to the windowsill, paused, then seemed to vault straight up, landing lightly on the ledge. "I put the cufflink in the dish in Uncle Lawrence's room and left." Nora's confident tone faltered. "I was halfway down the stairs when I decided to change my shoes. They were new, and they were pinching my toes terribly. I was climbing the stairs to return to my room, and that's when I saw Gilbert. I was still several steps down, and I'm sure my head was the only thing visible from down the hall—that's why Gilbert didn't notice me when he came out of Uncle Lawrence's room. Gilbert went back down the hall to his dressing room, so he didn't see me."

"Did you mention it to him when you changed your shoes?"

"No. I didn't want to speak to him." Nora examined the cuticle of her thumbnail. "Gilbert and I also had a little blowup that afternoon. He wasn't happy I'd tried to convince Uncle Lawrence to set us up in a flat again. I decided I'd rather wear uncomfortable shoes than talk to Gilbert right then."

"And you didn't just ask him about it later?"

"We weren't speaking. And there wasn't time the next day. Uncle Lawrence was . . . gone. It was terrible with the doctor and then the police in the house. That horrible inspector came—Thorn—and he talked to Gilbert and me at the same time. Gilbert said he didn't go into Uncle Lawrence's room *at all* that evening, so of course I couldn't contradict him. You can see that, can't you?"

My thoughts reeled. She suspected her husband had murdered her new father-in-law. No wonder she'd locked Gilbert out of her room.

I made a noise that could be interpreted as sympathetic. I didn't agree that I would have kept quiet, but I supposed she felt she was protecting herself.

Nora said, "The reporters were sniffing around constantly. You have no idea how persistent they can be."

I begged to differ. I knew Essie, after all, but I kept that thought to myself. I didn't want to derail Nora now that she seemed to be honestly recounting what had happened.

"So I decided if I dropped a tidbit of information about the mummy, it would be a good distraction." She lifted a shoulder. "It worked. The reporters fell over themselves to write about the mummy. The inquest was only mentioned in passing."

"What about all the recent stories about the curse? Why would you continue to feed stories to the newspapers?"

"Because that awful reporter who I spoke to the first time contacted me and told me if I didn't provide details for a new story about the mummy—well, he'd go to print with a story naming me as his source for all the details about the curse. I couldn't have that."

"Blackmail from a member of the press," I said. "Interesting."

Essie had said Charlie, the reporter writing the stories, was notoriously lazy. He must have decided it was easier to manufacture his stories than to find new stories to report on.

"Did you steal the amulets and jewelry from the mummy?" At this point I wouldn't put it past her to have staged the theft to create fodder for the newspaper stories.

A look of distaste passed over Nora's face. "No. I'd never touch something like that."

Her revulsion seemed genuine, and I thought she probably was telling the truth.

A tap on the door sounded, and a footman opened it. "Pardon me. Your taxi has arrived, Lady Mulvern."

"I'll be right down," Nora said. The footman withdrew but left the door open. Nora stood. "I consider everything I've told you to be in the strictest confidence and expect you to keep it to yourself," she said as she swept out of the room.

She'd barely left before another footman returned. "Lady Agnes would like to speak to you in the morning room, Miss Belgrave."

CHAPTER TWENTY-THREE

I made my way to the morning room, barely noticing the opulent furnishings and decor. I'd been in Mulvern House long enough that they were becoming so familiar to me that their beauty didn't register. My thoughts were preoccupied with what Nora had told me. Nora wanted me to keep her secret, and I intended to do so—for now. I felt like a tiny light had been switched on, illuminating a small corner of a cavernous room. I needed to find out what the rest of the dark corners contained before I spoke to Lady Agnes.

I felt I was finally getting to the truth of what had happened the night Lord Mulvern died, but Nora had lied to me once, and Gilbert had apparently done the same. Before I went to Lady Agnes with any updates on what I'd discovered, I wanted to check Nora's story.

I tapped on the open door to the morning room and entered. "Good afternoon, Miss Belgrave," Lady Agnes said. "I've written you a check." She came across the room, a slip of paper in hand. "It's the balance of the amount that we agreed upon. I can't thank you enough for what you've done."

I looked up from the check. "What I've done?"

"Without you asking questions, Mr. Nunn's activities never would have come to light."

"I'm afraid I don't understand. There's no solid proof that Mr. Nunn killed your uncle."

A wrinkle appeared between Lady Agnes's eyebrows. Now that she was closer to me, I noticed her eyes were red and her eyelids were puffy. She'd been crying. "We have Mr. Nunn's confession thanks to you. It's a tragic and sad situation." She looked away and pressed her fingers to the bridge of her nose as she fought off tears. "Terribly sorry," she said as she took a deep breath. "But now that we know what happened, I find myself a tad emotional." She sniffed and straightened her shoulders. "But at least I know what happened, which—although disturbing—gives us a resolution. I'm a firm believer in knowing the truth, even if it's uncomfortable or difficult. We have that truth now. Mr. Nunn wasn't what we thought, but at least we know what happened."

"But it was my understanding Inspector Longly is still investigating Mr. Nunn's death."

"Still investigating? What is there to investigate?"

"Perhaps Mr. Nunn was only a convenient scapegoat," I said, knowing I was overstepping, all thoughts of being circumspect disappearing. Lady Agnes had essentially said my work was done. Next, she'd tell me to pack my bags and walk me to the door.

"No, I'm sure that's not the case. Mr. Nunn was

desperate. He didn't want to face the loss of his job. He was here in Mulvern House the night Uncle Lawrence died, and he wrote a letter confessing to the deed. No, I'm sure Mr. Nunn was responsible, and he took his own life out of regret."

How ironic. Lady Agnes had been so adamant her uncle's death hadn't been suicide, but she was quick to accept the explanation of suicide for Nunn's death. Clearly, she wanted answers about her uncle's death so badly that she'd accepted this solution and was clinging to it.

"But there are still so many questions—"

"No," Lady Agnes said, her tone unyielding. "There are no more questions, at least none that concern you, Miss Belgrave."

She wouldn't change her mind. Anything I said from this moment on would only dig me further into the hole I'd just begun digging when I challenged her thoughts. I held out the check to her. "I can't accept this."

"Of course you can. I wanted answers about my uncle's death, and I have them now." She gave me a brief, strained smile then walked back to her desk. "I won't accept it back. It's yours. Keep it or destroy it as you like, but I always pay my debts."

I recognized a stubborn streak in Lady Agnes that I possessed as well. In fact, interacting with her now was a bit like looking in a mirror. I knew she wouldn't change her mind, so I folded the check in half and put it in my pocket. I wouldn't deposit it, and I wouldn't stop looking for the truth about Lord Mulvern's death. Even though Lady Agnes considered the matter settled, it didn't mean it was.

The telephone on her desk rang, and Lady Agnes said, "I do hope you'll stay on with us at least until tomorrow and attend the exhibit opening, then I'm sure you have obligations you must attend to."

Ah, manners—only those of the best breeding can inform you their hospitality toward you has ended but couch it in a way that makes it sound as if you're doing them a favor. Well, I was as much of a lady as Lady Agnes and could match her display of decorum. "I would like that," I said. I'd stay on until the next day and use every moment of my time at Mulvern House to continue my investigation on my own.

CHAPTER TWENTY-FOUR

I was on my way to the drawing room before dinner later that evening when I heard my name. I turned around. Gilbert stood in the doorway of the billiard room, which I'd just passed. "A word, Miss Belgrave, before we go into the drawing room."

"Of course," I said, but I felt a new wariness toward him since my conversation with Nora. Yet he looked exactly the same. He had the same open, rather vacant expression, and his clothes, while of the best cut, couldn't erase his slapdash style. His tie was off center and wrinkles already creased one of his lapels. He gestured for me to precede him into the billiard room, and my hesitation melted away.

He must've been practicing. Three billiard balls ranged over the table, and a cue stick rested on the table. He closed the door, which would have made me nervous, except there was a second door that stood open to the library. I didn't take a seat but leaned on the edge of the billiard table.

Gilbert went around to the opposite side of the table and picked up a billiard ball. "I understand you've upset my wife, Miss Belgrave."

"Nora told you of our conversation?"

Gilbert put the ball back on the table and gave it a shove. It raced across the smooth surface and hit another ball with a *thwack*. "No. But I know Nora's moods. I spoke to her briefly before she left this afternoon, and she was quite upset. She'd just come from speaking to you. You've probably noted Nora isn't a deep sort of person. Therefore, you must be the problem."

I could either deny it or challenge him. It might be my only chance to confront him with what I'd learned. My stay at Mulvern House would end after tomorrow. "I'm not the source of her upset—you are."

Gilbert paused as he reached for another billiard ball. "Me?"

"Yes. She's concerned about you."

He stretched across the table for the other ball. "She has an interesting way of showing it."

I picked up one of the cue sticks from the rack. It had been years since I'd played billiards. Jasper, Peter, Gwen, and I had played on rainy days at Parkview, but I didn't have any interest playing the game now. The frisson of nervousness I'd felt about talking with Gilbert had returned. There was an aggressiveness—or perhaps a frustration, I wasn't sure which—in his attitude that I hadn't seen before. I felt better with something heavy in my hands. "Why did you go into your uncle's room the evening he died?"

Gilbert spun the billiard ball on the table, his hand making a quick rotation each time it began to slow down. "I didn't."

"You were seen."

He continued to spin the billiard ball, but his gaze dropped from mine.

"Right now, your sister thinks Mr. Nunn was responsible for your uncle's death, but I do have to wonder if perhaps Mr. Nunn is taking the blame for someone else."

He looked up, a question in his expression.

"Perhaps for you," I said, my palms going sweaty. The cue stick felt slippery, and I tightened my grip.

"Hold up. You think—" He stepped back from the table. "You think *I* killed Uncle Lawrence . . . and also had something to do with Nunn's death?" He turned away, then spun back. "That's what you're insinuating, isn't it? That I killed Uncle Lawrence, then killed Nunn to cover it up?"

He looked absolutely stunned at the idea. Was I wrong? I'd thought he might be guilty, but unless he was a consummate actor, I didn't see how he could be so convincing in his bewilderment. He paced back and forth along the billiard table, then turned to me. "I loved my uncle, Miss Belgrave," he said with a tremble in his voice. "That's not a sentiment most men will express, but I'll gladly own up to it. Uncle Lawrence took in my sister and me and cared for us. Yes, Uncle Lawrence and I had some disagreements, but I would never—*never*—do anything to hurt him." Certainty reverberated through his words.

"I believe you." It wasn't so much his passionate defense that had convinced me, but his sheer befuddlement at the idea he was a murderer. "But then why did you lie?"

Gilbert leaned forward and gripped the edge of the billiard table. "To protect someone. Someone very dear to me."

"It was for Nora, wasn't it?" I asked, the words popping out as it came to me. I was sure the only two people who Gilbert would consider dear to him were Lady Agnes and Nora. "You saw Nora go into your uncle's room, and she saw you leave the room," I said as I worked it out. "But you've both been idiots and haven't talked to each other. You've spent the intervening weeks suspecting each other."

Gilbert paced around the table, closing the distance between us. Before he reached me, I whipped the cue stick up and gave him a good poke in the middle, which blew the air out of his lungs and allowed me to continue. "Neither one of you did it. Nora went into the room to return a cufflink she found. You saw her but didn't say anything, then she came back upstairs and saw you leave the room."

Gilbert gripped the billiard table and sucked in a noisy breath. "Nora went into the room to return a cufflink?"

"Yes, she found it on the floor in the hall. Or that's what she says."

Gilbert closed his eyes briefly as he braced his arm on the billiard table. He was relieved, I realized. "I didn't see her, but I could smell her lily of the valley scent when I went into the room. I knew she'd been in there."

"But why did *you* go into the room?"

"Nora and Uncle Lawrence had had a—um—a tiff earlier in the day, but you probably know all about that too, I imagine, since you seem to know everything else. Yes, I thought so. I wanted to smooth things over. I thought Uncle Lawrence might be in his dressing room. I wanted to catch him before he went down to dinner, but his room and dressing room were empty. And before you ask, I did not approach the bedside table. I didn't touch anything."

"Then you need to speak to Nora and tell her exactly what happened."

"Right. Yes, you're exactly right," he said, his face taking on a look of happiness. I knew he wasn't even thinking about me as he brushed past me and hurried out the door. I replaced the cue stick in the rack and followed Gilbert to the drawing room.

I reached it just as he took a seat on the sofa beside Nora, who had been flipping through a magazine. She pulled back from him, but Gilbert leaned in and spoke quickly in a low voice. I couldn't hear what he was saying, but the range of emotions flitting across Nora's face went from wariness to surprise to relief.

She tossed the magazine down and swiveled so she faced him. She answered him, also in muted tones.

Lady Agnes and I had to carry the conversation that evening at dinner. She behaved perfectly correctly toward me, but there was a reserved veneer to her manner where I was concerned. However, we conversed on a range of topics. Gilbert and Nora exchanged long gazes and continually missed picking up threads of conversation that had to be repeated for them. If what they'd said was true, if they were simply covering for each other out of misplaced loyalty, then neither one of them had put the sleeping powders in the tumbler on Lord Mulvern's bedside table, which left me with hardly any suspects at all.

CHAPTER TWENTY-FIVE

*W*hen I set out from Mulvern House the next morning, the fog had thinned. Instead of the almost impenetrable murky gray gloom that had smothered the city, reducing visibility to a few feet, the fog was now a wispy mist with a pearlescent quality, and I could see several yards down the path as I made my way across Hyde Park.

I'd decided I had to confirm what Nora and Gilbert had told me about the night their uncle had died. It certainly seemed as if they were lovebirds and all was well in their world, but I couldn't simply accept what they had said without double checking. I could think of only one person who might be able to verify their stories. The previous night after dinner, I'd written a note to Hodges, telling him I had a few more questions and that I'd come by for a visit in the morning and hoped that was convenient.

I hadn't received a reply, and as I tapped on his door, I knew he might be out or turn me away. But

Hodges opened the door. "Good morning, Miss Belgrave. Won't you come in?"

His manner was still reserved, but his greeting was considerably more welcoming than the last time I had visited him. He even smiled as he gestured for me to precede him down the hall. "Thank you for seeing me," I said. "I apologize for the short notice."

"It's no inconvenience at all. Mother will be delighted to see you again. Would you care for a cup of tea or coffee?"

"No, thank you," I said as I entered the sitting room, which hadn't changed at all since my last visit, except that Mrs. Hodges was now working on a piece of knitting made with yellow yarn. I took out the ball of pale blue yarn I'd bought on my way over. "Hello, Mrs. Hodges. I've brought you some wool."

She put her knitting needles down and ran her gnarled fingers over the wool with a feather-light touch. "Now this is a fine shade of blue. Blue is my favorite color, you know."

"I'm glad you like it."

Mrs. Hodges pulled a basket into her lap and dug around in it. By the time I took a seat on the sofa, she'd already found a new set of needles and had begun to work with the blue yarn.

"That was very thoughtful, Miss Belgrave," Hodges said as he sat down in a chair across from me.

"I'm glad she liked it. Now, I don't want to take up too much of your morning, so I'll come directly to the point. I have a few questions I hope you can help me with."

"I'm happy to help in any way I can."

"Thank you. First, do you remember if Lord Mulvern lost a cufflink shortly before he died?"

Obviously, the question wasn't what Hodges expected. He tilted his head to the side, eyes narrowed. "Indeed I do. It happened the day before Lord Mulvern passed. He went down to dinner, wearing his diamond and ruby cufflinks, but when he came back after dinner, he was missing one. We searched the room, the dining room, the drawing room—all over the house, in fact. But we didn't find it."

"Did it ever turn up?"

Hodges's eyes narrowed even more. "Yes. Interestingly, I found it the next night—the night Lord Mulvern passed. He'd already gone down to dinner. I went downstairs to retrieve the handkerchiefs, and when I returned, I found the cufflink in the dish on his bureau. I put it away in its proper place and didn't think about it again until you mentioned it now. It was rather odd, it reappearing that way."

"And when you came back into the room and found the cufflink, was that also when you noticed the scent of lily of the valley?"

"Why, yes, it was."

"Thank you, that's helpful. Just a few more questions. Did Gilbert ever stop by Lord Mulvern's room to visit with his uncle?"

"Yes. It wasn't a frequent occurrence, but it happened occasionally," Hodges said. "From the time he and his sister were children, they often visited Lord and Lady Mulvern in their chambers. Lord and Lady Mulvern's suite wasn't off-limits."

"So it wouldn't be unusual for Gilbert to step in to see his uncle on his way down to dinner?"

"No, not at all."

"I see. One other thing. Did Lord Mulvern use the desk in his room to answer correspondence?"

Hodges nodded. "If it was a personal note, he'd use the desk. If it was a business matter, he'd delegate that to Mr. Nunn." Hodges permitted himself a small smile. "Lord Mulvern's penmanship was not the best, and he used to go through quite a few sheets of paper before he achieved a perfectly written note. He found it a great annoyance to reply to messages and invitations himself, but he often felt the note should come from his pen, not Mr. Nunn's."

"Thank you, Mr. Hodges. What you've told me is very useful. I won't take up any more of your time." I stood and said goodbye to Mrs. Hodges. She nodded in time with her rocking chair, never missing a stitch as she transformed the pale blue yarn into a swath of fabric that was already several inches wide.

As we walked down the short hallway, Hodges said to me, "I was sorry to hear what happened with young Mr. Nunn."

"You read about it in the paper?" I hadn't checked the newspapers that morning. I'd been so intent on seeing Hodges that I'd breakfasted quickly and hadn't even glanced at them. I hadn't bought a paper from a newsboy on my walk either.

"Yes. Quite a tragedy."

I agreed, but beyond that, I kept silent. I didn't think it wise to share my suspicions about Nunn's death.

Hodges reached for the doorknob. "Are you making progress with your inquiries?"

"I believe I am. Some things have become clearer, and the information you gave me today has clarified a few more things as well. I'm afraid I can't say more than that at the moment, but I will let you know how things turn out."

"I would appreciate that."

We said goodbye, and I was already in the corridor outside the flat when another question came to me. I turned back before Hodges closed the door. "Oh, Mr. Hodges, one other thing—the new butler, Boggs. What did you think of him?" It might be a few more days before Lady Agnes received a reply from the Misses Piedmont, depending on how quickly they answered her letter. Boggs hadn't been in the breakfast room that morning, and when I had asked after him, the footman I had spoken to said Boggs was expected to be away for a few more days.

"I only worked with him a short time, but he seemed a decent fellow. Fair and concerned for the staff under him."

"What about how he went about his work?"

"He had his own way of doing things, some of it a bit . . . unusual, I'd say, but nothing that caused any problems."

"I see. Thank you again, Mr. Hodges," I said quickly and left before he could ask me why I wanted to know more about the butler. I wouldn't have been able to give him a good answer. I didn't know exactly what I was searching for related to Boggs.

I set off back across the park, the sun now a fuzzy

bright ball beyond the filter of the mist. I squinted against the growing brightness. The multitude of water droplets in the thinning fog seeming to magnify the sunlight that managed to penetrate the haziness. I decided I'd return to Mulvern House and see if Jasper had sent a telegram about Boggs.

If I didn't have a message from Jasper, I'd have to telephone him—something Jasper's man Grigsby, frowned upon—but I'd just have to brave the irritation of a perfect gentleman's gentleman to get the information I needed about Boggs. If Jasper hadn't made his way to the antique shop, I'd have to go myself that day.

As I walked, I debated if I could draw a mental line through two names on my suspect list, Gilbert and Nora. From all appearances, they seemed to have nothing to do with Lord Mulvern's death, but I'd learned appearances could be deceiving. Could I be completely wrong about them? Perhaps Gilbert and Nora had worked together to do away with Lord Mulvern, then they'd carefully orchestrated their behavior since then to make it appear they suspected each other.

I shook my head. It was a preposterous idea—and one that didn't quite make sense. Who would they have been preforming for in the weeks before I arrived? Lady Agnes? Would they have gone to all the effort of the charade when Lord Mulvern's death was already categorized as a suicide? It would be an awful lot of work for an uninterested audience.

I rounded the corner of the park in Mulvern Square. The fog had lifted to the point that I could actually see Mulvern House from several yards away. Through the mist, I was able to distinguish Jasper's figure with his wavy fair hair under his dark hat as he strolled up the drive.

"Jasper," I called and hurried up the circular drive to meet him before he reached the porte-cochère.

"Hello, Olive. I was just coming to visit you, old bean."

"You have news?"

"I'll say. Are you free for a spot of lunch?"

"Definitely."

I threaded my hand through his arm when he offered his elbow, and we set off back down the drive. "What did you have in mind?"

"Not the Savoy, I'm afraid," he said. "I have a young man who is meeting me at a pub not too far from here."

"A young man?"

"An informative fellow, especially compared to his colleagues. I wasn't able to get much out of the chaps at the antique shop, but the lad, who is thirteen, is employed there three days a week."

"What did he have to say?"

"I'd rather have him tell you in his own words."

"My, that makes me worry a bit."

"I feel it's a good test of his story. I'll be interested to see how much it changes when he repeats it."

"You don't trust him?"

"I do, but it never hurts to double check."

"My thoughts exactly," I said and brought him up to date on what had happened the night before and during my visit with Hodges. By the time I'd finished, we'd reached the pub.

"So you think Gilbert and Nora didn't do it?"

"It appears that way."

Jasper opened the door, letting out a burst of sound mingled with cigarette smoke. Jasper had to duck underneath the low lintel, but it wasn't a problem for me. He nodded across the smoky room. "Well, the lad has passed the first test. He's here."

"He looks respectable," I said, taking in his clothes, which were a bit threadbare but clean and well pressed. He'd removed a flat cap and clutched it, his fingers kneading the fabric. A swath of reddish-brown hair fell over his eyes, but he twitched the fringe off his face with a quick jerk of his head when he spotted Jasper.

As we made our way across the pub to him, Jasper said in a low voice, "I looked into his background. Bobby's father died on the Somme. His mother takes in laundry while he works at the antique shop three days a week."

"Oh, how sad," was all I had time to say. That sketchy outline of Bobby's past was a story that was too common nowadays. An achy feeling settled around my heart as I took in his wide dark eyes and freckled nose.

Jasper made the introductions, and I put on a bright smile. Considering I'd just met Bobby, an expression of sympathy about his situation would be inappropriate, so I squashed down my feelings of commiseration.

Bobby had excellent manners. He greeted me politely, and, following Jasper's lead, he waited for me to be seated first at the table. Once we'd all ordered the plowman's lunch, Jasper turned to the young man. "Bobby, I'd like for you to tell my friend exactly what you told me."

His Adam's apple surged up and down as his gaze went from me to Jasper. "You mean about the shop?"

"Yes," I said. "What do you do at the antique shop?"

His shoulders relaxed, and I could tell he was comfortable answering that question. "I sweep, clean the glass cabinets, and wrap up whatever people buy."

"Mr. Boggs must trust you."

"I suppose." Bobby looked to Jasper. "Do you want me to tell her about the bloke who brought in the Egyptian stuff?"

"Yes, do."

"There's this old man," Bobby said with another twitch of his head to remove his fringe from his eyes. "He has white hair, and he works at one of those fancy houses. He brings in Egyptian things and sells them to Mr. Boggs."

I exchanged a glance with Jasper. Boggs was the only gray-headed person at Mulvern House.

I asked, "What sort of Egyptian things?"

He shrugged one shoulder. "You know, stuff like they find in the pyramids and tombs and things. Statues and jars and little rocks carved to look like bugs."

Jasper took out a notebook and handed it to me. "Bobby sketched a few of the things he remembered."

I pressed the notebook on the table, running my hand down the crease to keep it open. "Oh my," I breathed. I was far from an expert in Egyptian antiquities, but many of the drawings looked similar to the items I'd seen in the grand gallery.

Bobby's stubby finger touched a rough sketch of a statue of a cat. "That one had a collar of gold with green stones. And these—" His finger shifted to a row of four jars with lids shaped like human and animal heads. "They were made of a white stone that you could almost see through. Mr. Boggs said I had to be careful with them because they were valuable."

"And this man who brings in the Egyptian items, does the owner of the shop know him?"

"I'll say. He's a relation of Mr. Boggs's. It makes the whole thing confusing to have two people named Mr. Boggs."

"I'm sure it does," I said, but my thoughts were elsewhere. Servants not only knew a great deal about the family—their habits and foibles—but they were also entrusted with the care of costly jewelry, art, and antiquities. I tried to imagine Brimble, the butler at Parkview Hall, nicking belongings from my aunt and uncle . . . no, it wouldn't happen. Brimble would never break the bond of trust between himself and the family. "How long has this been going on?" I asked Bobby.

He lifted a shoulder. "A couple of months, I suppose. But it's been a while since I've seen the old man. Mr. Boggs—the owner, that is—was saying the other day he'd like to have more stuff from Mulvern House because it was easy to sell with its . . . um . . . pro—, provo—" He frowned.

"Provenance?" Jasper asked.

"Yes, sir. That's exactly what he said."

So not only was Boggs stealing from the family, his relative was touting the items as having come from Mulvern House, a good provenance, which I was sure increased their value.

Our food arrived and Bobby tucked into his meal, all his hesitation and awkwardness dropping away. We talked of London and the foggy weather while we ate. As soon as his plate was clear, Bobby glanced at the clock behind the bar. "Thank you for lunch, sir."

"You're welcome, Bobby. I appreciate you repeating your story for my friend."

Bobby squeezed his cap. "I'd best get on. I have to be at the shop soon."

"Off you go, then," Jasper said.

Bobby ducked his head at me. "Madam," he said, then darted away through the crowded room.

"Did his story match up?" I asked, watching Bobby's slight figure through the window as he passed by outside.

"Almost word for word."

"Then you think he's telling the truth—that Boggs is bringing antiquities from Mulvern House and selling them to his relative."

"It appears that way, yes."

"It would explain why Boggs—the butler Boggs—has disappeared." On our walk to the pub, I'd told Jasper that Boggs hadn't returned. "Perhaps Boggs suspected he was about to be found out and made up the story about his sick mother."

"I believe you're right." The notebook was still open on the table, and Jasper plucked it up and flipped to a new page. "After I spoke with Bobby yesterday, I toddled over to Somerset House and looked up some records. Purely out of curiosity." Jasper shot me a glance out of the corner of his eye. "This curiosity thing must be catching."

"No!" I said in mock horror. "You, man about town, so blasé and bored, actually interested in something besides the cut of your suit or color of your waistcoat?"

"Don't be silly. Grigsby attends to my wardrobe. I never waste a thought on what I'm wearing."

"I don't believe that for a moment, but now you've piqued *my* curiosity. What did you find?" I strained to read over his shoulder. "It must be interesting."

"Rather. I looked up the birth certificate of the antique shop owner, Samuel Boggs. He was born in 1886 in Dover, which gave me the name of his parents, Timothy and Susanna Boggs. A little more exploration of the archives turned up Samuel's brother, Fredrick."

"*Brother*? Are you sure? I thought the antique shop owner was Boggs's nephew—or perhaps grandson. Although, Lady Agnes mentioned the butler's first name the other day, and it *was* Fredrick. Perhaps Fredrick is a common name in the family?"

"No, I couldn't find another Fredrick Boggs," Jasper said. "More interestingly, Susanna Boggs died in 1905, also in Dover."

"So Boggs wasn't called away to visit his sick mother's bedside in Northumberland or anywhere else."

"It appears not."

The fact that Boggs's story didn't hold up didn't surprise me. What was truly odd was the news that Fredrick Boggs, the butler, and Samuel Boggs, the antique shop owner, were brothers. "Perhaps they had different mothers . . . ? Could that account for the age difference?"

"No. The names of the parents are the same for both boys." Jasper pressed the notebook down on the table and pointed a manicured fingernail at a date. "Look at Fredrick Boggs's birth year."

"1891?" I asked, my glance traveling from the notebook to Jasper, who was nodding.

"Correct. I checked it twice."

"That can't be right," I said, but Jasper's neat printing was impeccable. "That makes Fredrick Boggs . . . thirty-two years old."

"Quite. You always were good at maths. It seems your aged butler is not who he says he is."

CHAPTER TWENTY-SIX

"I still find it hard to believe someone would impersonate a butler," I said as the taxi pulled up in front of Mulvern House.

Jasper paid the driver and held the door for me. "The position gives him the run of the house and authority over most of the staff."

"That's true, but think of all the work—managing the staff, overseeing every meal, keeping track of the wine and the pantry. When would he have the *time* to pilfer antiquities?"

"If the reward was great enough, I'm sure he fit it into his busy schedule. What are you going to do?" Jasper asked.

I looked at the front door of the grand house. "I have to tell Lady Agnes. She has to know that the person working for her isn't Frederick Boggs and that he's been spiriting Egyptian antiquities out of the town house and selling them to an antique shop." I blew out a breath and pressed a hand to my churning stomach. I dreaded imparting the news to Lady Agnes. I knew she wouldn't be pleased.

"Would you like me to come along?" Jasper asked.

"Yes, I would, especially since you're the one who consulted the records at Somerset House. Another question has just occurred to me," I said as we climbed the stairs to the front door. "Where is the real Frederick Boggs?"

"A very good question indeed."

Lady Agnes was at home, and we found her in the grand gallery, where she was directing two servants as they moved a new display case into alignment. "A little to the left . . . perfect. Now, fetch the last crate from the attic and bring it to the far end of the gallery," she instructed the footmen, then she caught sight of Jasper and me. "Miss Belgrave and Mr. Rimington, delighted to see you again," Lady Agnes said, coming across the room to greet us.

"The pleasure is all mine," Jasper said. I might be in Lady Agnes's bad books, but she wasn't holding my association with Jasper against him as she gave him a warm smile.

Jasper's gaze ranged over the gallery. "Wonderful place you have here."

"Thank you. It's currently not at its best," she said, gesturing to the crates and packing material scattered around the room. "With so many of our antiquities transferred to the museum for the exhibit, I'm filling the gaps here with a few things we normally keep in storage."

Many of the things Lady Agnes had pointed out to me on my first visit were gone, including several mummy coffins and the large pot her uncle had reconstructed from shards. I turned my attention to her. "I have a rather delicate matter to discuss with you," I said. "It's something you need to know."

Lady Agnes's wide smile vanished. "You sound quite serious."

"I'm afraid it is."

She glanced from me to Jasper.

"Mr. Rimington was influential in uncovering the information. I think he should be here as well," I added.

"Very well." She glanced at her watch. "But I can only give you a few moments. With the exhibit opening this evening, I have a full schedule today."

I took a deep breath and tried to ignore the churning in my stomach. Lady Agnes was already annoyed with me, but perhaps she'd appreciate the information I was about to share with her. Deep down, I knew that was a long shot, but Lady Agnes did need to know what I'd discovered about Boggs. "In the course of my inquiries into your uncle's death, I was curious about each person who had been at the house the evening he died, and that included your butler, Boggs."

"Of course."

"I discovered Boggs has ties to an antiques shop. At that time, I couldn't obtain any more information, but Jasper was able to speak to another employee of the shop and uncovered the fact that Boggs has been selling antiquities to the owner over the last several months."

"What?" Lady Agnes's gaze had strayed back to the far end of the gallery, but she whipped her head toward me.

Jasper held his notebook open to the page with the drawings.

I said, "It seems there's no question that the pieces were Egyptian antiquities, and it was general knowledge within the shop that they'd come from Mulvern House."

"Sell our antiquities? No, that's impos—" She broke off as she took the notebook and scanned the drawings. She took a few steps backward and ran her fingers through her hair, disarranging her curls.

"I'm afraid there's more."

"More?" Her arms dropped to her side, the notebook dangling from her hand.

"Jasper went to Somerset House to do research on Boggs's family. According to his birth certificate, Frederick Boggs is thirty-two years old."

"*Thirty-two?* But then—who is our gray-haired butler?"

"I'm not sure. And the other question is where is the thirty-two-year-old Frederick Boggs?"

I was about to launch into the details and tell her Boggs's mother had already passed on and that apparently the family resided in Dover, not Northumberland, but Lady Agnes snapped the notebook closed. "Come with me," she said as she shoved the book at Jasper. She set a brisk pace through the chain of rooms. Jasper and I followed in her wake. It reminded me of trying to keep up with Boggs when I'd trailed him to the antique shop.

We came to the morning room. Lady Agnes removed a set of keys from her desk drawer, turned on her heel, and went downstairs to the servants' hall. Jasper and I exchanged a look as we descended the stairs. The motion and activity in the servants' hall stopped as soon as we entered. Mrs. Ryan put her pen down on her desk and stood. "Lady Agnes—"

Lady Agnes waved her hand. "Do carry on, Mrs. Ryan. So sorry for the interruption, but I must retrieve something from the butler's pantry."

Lady Agnes's ringing tones sent the servants back to work. Mrs. Ryan slowly took her seat again, but she did glance over her shoulder several times as Lady Agnes selected the key from her ring and unlocked a door.

Jasper and I followed her inside the room, which was lined floor-to-ceiling with cabinetry. The upper cabinets had glass doors and held a range of silver serving dishes and expensive china. There was a small wooden sink lined with lead for washing up the delicate items, and a large table stretched down the middle of the room.

"This way." Lady Agnes moved around the corner to a small alcove, which contained an iron bedstead, a bureau, and a wardrobe. Lady Agnes went to the wardrobe and jerked the doors open. Over her shoulder, she said, "Mr. Rimington, you look in the bureau. Miss Belgrave, if you'd be so kind as to check under the bed . . . I'm sure if there's anything here, we'll find it quickly."

Lady Agnes worked through the small number of suits and shirts hanging in the wardrobe. Jasper lifted a shoulder and opened the top drawer of the bureau. I got down on my knees and looked under the bed. A small valise was pushed back against the wall. As I pulled it toward me, Jasper said, "How strange."

I sat back on my heels and waved away a pouf of

dust I'd stirred up. Jasper held a thick pile of envelopes fanned out as he read the addresses on each one. "These are all addressed to Mr. Frederick Boggs and go back at least ten years."

"So he's either been an imposter that long, or he got ahold of the real Fredrick Boggs's correspondence somehow," I said with a slightly sick feeling. I didn't want to think about how one came into possession of ten years' worth of another person's correspondence.

"Aha!" Lady Agnes stepped back from the wardrobe. She cradled two scarabs in her palm. They were both flat and oblong with shallow lines carved on the surface. One was a shade of pale turquoise, the other was black. "They were in the pocket of a pair of trousers at the back of the wardrobe." She positioned them on the bureau, then went back to her search.

I unfastened the straps of the valise. I wrinkled my nose at the strong antiseptic aroma as the case fell open, then I recoiled. A large amount of hair was squished in beside some ragged ties, a jar of face cream, and several worn collars. Then I realized the hair was a wig—a gray wig.

"Aggie, what on earth are you doing?"

All three of us turned to the door, where Gilbert stood, his gaze darting around the small room. "The footman at the door said you were below stairs . . ." His words trailed off as he spotted the scarabs.

Lady Agnes pointed to the scarabs. "Boggs is a thief. Miss Belgrave and her friend Mr. Rimington discovered the truth about him. Boggs has been taking things, probably from the attic, and selling them to an antique shop. No wonder he's disappeared, what with detective inspectors calling at all hours. I doubt his mother is unwell. Boggs was probably frightened he'd be found out and left."

Gilbert darted across the small room and bent over the scarabs. When he straightened, he looked as if he were about to be ill.

"Are you all right, Gilbert? Do you need to sit down a moment?" I asked.

"No." He cleared his throat, and it seemed he was forcing out his next words. "Aggie, Boggs is not a thief."

"What do you mean? I showed you the proof. It's right there on the bureau." Lady Agnes jerked a suit jacket out of the wardrobe and began turning out each pocket.

Gilbert briefly closed his eyes. "Those things were mine, Aggie. Anything Boggs has sold has been on my behalf."

Lady Agnes went still. "What?"

"I commissioned him to sell some items—all my own pieces—that Uncle Lawrence had given to me."

"But why? Why would you do that?"

Gilbert sent an embarrassed glance at Jasper and me as he strained his neck to one side and tugged at his collar, "Nora and I—well, you know we're not the most thrifty of people. We tend to get carried away. I'm afraid things got out of hand financially. Uncle Lawrence wouldn't cover the debts. I had to do something. I asked Boggs if he'd find somewhere to sell the pieces. He said he'd take care of it. I gave Boggs several small items, and he returned with cash, so I gave him a few more." Jasper nodded to the scarabs. "He quite liked those, and I gave them to him to keep . . . as a sort of tip."

"I see." Lady Agnes searched Gilbert's face for a moment, then sighed. "You could have come to me."

"No, I couldn't," he said with a finality in his tone that surprised me. Gilbert had struck me as someone whose standards were malleable, but apparently there were some lines he wouldn't cross.

"Well, then, at least our butler hasn't been stealing from us," Lady Agnes said. "But why do the records at Somerset House indicate Boggs is in his early thirties, not his sixties?"

"Boggs? Thirty?" Gilbert asked, his eyes widening.

"According to his birth certificate, Fredrick Boggs is thirty-two," Jasper said.

"Good grief," Gilbert said. "Then who is our butler?"

"Was our butler," Lady Agnes said. "I suppose that's something for Inspector Longly." Lady Agnes handed the scarabs to Gilbert. "You'd better take these. It doesn't look as if Boggs—or whoever he is—will return." Lady Agnes returned the suit jacket to the wardrobe, and Jasper replaced the letters and closed the bureau drawer.

"I think . . ." I said, then fell silent as Lady Agnes sent me a look that had me pressing my lips together. She didn't want to hear any more opinions from me. I hadn't exposed a thief in their house. Instead, I'd uncovered an embarrassing situation within their family. Lady Agnes had hired me to help her handle a delicate issue quietly, not expose awkward issues within the family.

I fastened the straps on the valise and shoved it under the bed. I had an idea of what had happened with Boggs, but I wasn't going to launch into it now. I wasn't about to make another statement to Lady Agnes without thoroughly checking it first. Being proven wrong once in a day was quite enough, and Lady Agnes's lips were pressed together in disapproval.

She shut the wardrobe door. "Miss Belgrave," she said, her voice tight. "I must ask you to stop interfering with things here at Mulvern House." She swept out the door and disappeared up the stairs to the main part of the house with Gilbert at her side.

I followed more slowly. Jasper held the green baize door for me, then fell into step behind me.

"I won't have a recommendation from Lady Agnes coming my way after this," I said.

"Buck up, old thing. I have no doubt you'll win her over in the end. And you are making progress in sorting out the muddle here at Mulvern House."

"Do you really think so? I feel as if I unpicked a knot or two but only created a worse tangle."

CHAPTER TWENTY-SEVEN

I was relieved when I walked into the drawing room that evening and saw Dorothy Gill, Nora's friend, had already arrived and was chatting away to both Nora and Lady Agnes. The arrangements were for Lady Agnes and Gilbert to go to the exhibit opening in the motor driven by their chauffeur. Dorothy and I would follow in a taxi.

I took a seat on the sofa beside Dorothy. "Good evening, ladies." With Dorothy between Lady Agnes and myself, we could avoid any awkwardness. Dorothy's dress was a simple sheath with a single thin line of beading along its wide bateau neckline. She wore an Egyptian-inspired turban with a long beaded fringe of gold, green, and red that framed her face and hung almost below her chin.

The fringe clattered as Dorothy swung around, bouncing on the sofa. "Hello, Miss Belgrave. Oh, what a lovely frock. That shade of blue brings out your eyes."

The velvet bodice on my dress was intricately

beaded, and I'd thought it might be too dressy for the event, but compared to Dorothy's turban headdress, I looked positively plain. Before I could return the compliment, Dorothy said, "Isn't this exciting? I've never been to a private opening of a museum exhibit." She whipped back to Lady Agnes, which sent the fringe flying. "I can't imagine speaking in front of everyone. I used to freeze up when the teacher called on me to read aloud in class. How are you so calm?"

"It's just a short welcome speech, nothing grand," Lady Agnes said, looking up from the notecard she'd been skimming. Her tone was light, but she flexed the notecard back and forth, and I could see the edges of it were worn. Lady Agnes wore an elegant chiffon frock in jade green with masses of tiny gold beads accenting the V-neck. The skirt fit snugly at her hips but flared out at the hem, reminiscent of the silhouettes of graceful Egyptian ladies on the pottery I'd seen in the grand gallery.

Gilbert entered the room, and Nora reached out a hand to him. He greeted us all, then pulled a chair closer to Nora and murmured something low in her ear, which brought a smile to her face. A look of disgruntlement flashed across Dorothy's face as she watched Nora and Gilbert. It appeared the new closeness between Gilbert and Nora was pushing Dorothy to the side. She seemed to sense her status had changed and wasn't happy about it.

A footman arrived and announced the motor and taxi were waiting. We moved to the entrance hall and were being helped into our coats when Dorothy picked up Nora's handbag, which she'd put down on a table while she buttoned her coat. Dorothy held the purse out. "Don't forget your handbag like you did in the taxi that evening." It seemed to be a verbal tug on Nora's sleeve, a little reminder that Dorothy had been helpful to her in the past and that she didn't want to be overlooked now.

Nora rolled her eyes as she took the handbag strap. "Good grief. I'll never live that down." Nora threaded her arm through Gilbert's elbow and stalked away. As we crossed the porte-cochère, Nora looked over her shoulder, her chin tucked into the collar of her mink. "You made sure I got it back. All's well that ends well." Her sharp tone implied, *and don't mention it again.*

Nora, Gilbert, and Lady Agnes climbed into the motor, while Dorothy and I got into the taxi. Dorothy threw herself back against the cushion, the fringe on her turban swinging against her cheeks and framing her disgruntled expression. "She acts as if it was my fault! She forgot it, not me." Dorothy adjusted the lapels of her wool broadcloth coat. "Now Nora will be huffy all night," she added in a sulky tone. "And it was only because of Mr. Dennett that she got it back, anyway. He found it after they left the nightclub, but she'd never be cross with *him*."

"I don't understand."

"We all shared a taxi when we left the Bluebird—the nightclub," she added when she saw my confusion. "Mr. Dennett, Aggie, Gilbert, Nora and me. It was quite a crush. The taxi went to Mulvern House first. I was next to be dropped off, and it was only when Mr. Dennett was getting out of the taxi at his lodgings that he found Nora's handbag squished down in the seat.

He was leaving town and didn't have time to return it to Nora, but I live just around the corner from him, so he dropped it with me the next day, and I gave it back to her. Nora should be thanking me, not grousing at me." The taxi swung across the road and pulled up at the museum. "Oh, look at her coat," Dorothy said, gazing at a woman down the road who was getting into a taxi. "Wouldn't a full-length mink be divine in this weather?"

"Um, yes. It would certainly be warm," I said. A full-length fur of any sort was out of my budget and probably Dorothy's as well, but fur coats were far from my thoughts. I grabbed her sleeve to prevent her from climbing out of the taxi. "The nightclub they visited, was it the club's opening night?"

"Yes, it was the Bluebird Club. Were you there?"

"No, I wasn't," I said as we climbed out of the taxi and made our way into the museum. I was lost in my thoughts, and everything around me seemed hazy. Dorothy chattered on about furs as we dropped off our coats, then we rejoined Lady Agnes, Gilbert, and Nora at the entrance to the gallery where the exhibit had been set up.

"Nicely done, Aggie," Gilbert said as he looked up to the fabric banner draped over the lintel, which read *The Mulvern Collection.* "Uncle Lawrence would like that."

"Thank you, Gilbert. I'm glad you think so," Lady Agnes said. We passed under the banner into the large, high-ceilinged room. Rows of mummy coffins positioned so they stood upright lined both sides of the long room, and two actual mummies lay within their glass cases at the center of the room. I imagined those would draw the most interest. More display cabinets ranged around the room, and I wondered if any of the cabinets were from Lord Mulvern's special order. As I surveyed the room, I was able to recognize the contents of several of the cabinets, which held scarabs, pottery, tools, and jewelry. The larger pots and statues stood on plinths and were interspersed between the cases. I realized one of them was the pot Lord Mulvern had reassembled from shards.

We'd been among the first arrivals, but Rathburn was at the far end of the room talking to a waiter, and Mr. Dennett stood in front of the mummy coffins, a cigarette in one hand and drink in the other. His color was high, and his gaze followed our group as we moved into the room. I watched Mr. Dennett as he tossed back his drink, my thoughts clicking away.

Lady Agnes went to speak to Rathburn, and Dorothy went to one of the glass cases. "Miss Belgrave," she said in a tone that indicated it was not the first time she'd called my name. "You must see this."

I shook off my contemplative state. I was at a fabulous soirée. It was bad manners to stand alone and simply think. I could mull things over later. The idea that I'd had—well, it required some serious thought, and I couldn't do that in the middle of a social event. I joined Dorothy and peered into the case, which contained a wide semi-circular collar made of thousands of tiny tubular beads in a greenish turquoise color.

"Isn't this spectacular? Wouldn't it be just too, too lovely to wear something like that?"

A masculine voice sounded behind us. "I say, you'd probably have to be dead to wear it."

We both turned, and I said, "Jasper! I didn't know you'd be here."

"Oh, didn't I mention it? I accepted the invitation ages ago. No one can resist mummies."

Dorothy turned back to the jewelry. "Are you sure? About it being only worn by a mummy?"

Jasper said, "According to the helpful little card there, it's a funerary ornament found within the wrappings of a mummy."

Dorothy's nose wrinkled. "Oh. But why wouldn't they have worn it when they were alive? It's so beautiful. It seems a shame to cover it up in layers of cloth."

"I don't know. I'm sure Lady Agnes could tell you."

"Yes, you're right." Dorothy headed for Lady Agnes, and I said to Jasper, "I don't think Lady Agnes will thank you for that."

He waved his hand. "Lady Agnes can handle Dorothy." Jasper plucked two champagne glasses off the tray of a passing waiter and handed one to me. "Shall we have a look at the antiquities?"

"Yes, let's." Guests were arriving and the room was filling up. The noise level had risen, a growing burble of sound that echoed off the high ceiling and marble walls. We circulated through the displays, pausing by mummies, pottery, and statues, but my attention was not on the displays. I'd tried to put my mad notion aside to consider later, but the idea wouldn't go away. I was busy sorting through several bits of information I'd picked up over the last week, arranging each shard of information, turning it one way, then another in my mind, like Lord Mulvern must have done with the broken pottery pieces. I had a glimmer of an idea that let me arrange the fragments into a pattern that made sense, but it was such an incredible idea that I didn't want to say it aloud.

". . . don't you think so?"

I gave a little start and looked at Jasper. "I'm sorry, I missed what you said. I'm a bit preoccupied."

"No matter. Care to talk about it? I *am* your Watson, remember?"

"You're much more than Watson," I said, squeezing his arm.

"Well, there's no excuse, then. What has you wool-gathering instead of listening to my sparkling conversation?"

I smiled at his mocking tone. "Sorry to have missed your repartee. I'm sure you'll tell me about it later." One of the waiters circled by, and I strained on tiptoe to look over Jasper's shoulder.

"Something interesting behind me?" Jasper swiveled around.

I pointed with the rim of my glass. "That waiter there. Do you see him? The one with the dark hair? He looks like . . . Boggs. It *is* Boggs, but without the gray hair and wrinkles." So I had been right, at least about one thing. I set my glass down and pushed through the crowd. I managed to catch the man by the sleeve before he disappeared through a doorway at one corner of the room with his empty tray.

CHAPTER TWENTY-EIGHT

"*B*oggs?" The lighting in the gallery wasn't strong, but I was close enough to see I was right. His hair was black, and the deep lines on either side of his mouth and across his forehead were smoothed out, but his features were the same. "It is you."

The door beside him opened and a waiter came out with a tray of hors d'oeuvres. Boggs stepped to the side, a resigned look on his face. "Yes, Miss Belgrave. How can I help you?"

"Perfect manners even when you're not a butler? No wonder you did so well in the role. Why did you dress as an old man when you're clearly a fit, younger man? Why the masquerade?"

Boggs glanced at Jasper, who'd arrived at my side. Jasper gave Boggs a long look, then said to me, "Fredrick Boggs isn't missing, is he?"

"No. He was impersonating an aged butler, and he was just about to tell me why he did it."

For a second I thought Boggs would dodge away through the door, but he folded the tray to his chest and said with a sigh, "Jobs are hard to come by now, miss. You may not know that, but it's true."

"I completely understand that. But I don't understand the makeup and the wig."

"People expect a certain . . . gravitas—a presence—from a butler. He must be distinguished. I'm too young to be distinguished." He waved a hand at his smooth countenance and thick black hair.

"But if you had experience—oh, I see," I said as his face closed down. "You didn't have experience but wanted the job."

He squared his shoulders. "I had plenty of experience. Well, experience of a sort."

"What do you mean? Were you a footman?"

"No, a butler." One corner of his mouth turned up, and a mischievousness appeared in his eyes that I'd never seen when he was in his role of butler at Mulvern House. "On stage."

"You played a butler on stage and thought you could land a job in a great house in real life from your stage experience?" I asked. "No wonder you forged your letter of reference."

His chest expanded. "I didn't forge anything. I merely listed the Misses Piedmont as a referral. If they failed to reply to questions from an agency . . . well, I couldn't help that, could I?"

When I'd recognized the hair in the valise was a wig and smelled the distinctive aroma of cosmetics, I'd suspected Boggs was a younger man, not an older one. It explained why his hair was crookedly parted on the morning of the break-in. In his hurry to get upstairs, he'd put his wig on off-center. His rapid walking pace and pale hands, which were free from liver spots, should have clued me in sooner. I glanced back to the room, wondering how long we had before Lady Agnes began her welcome speech. I still had so many questions. His story still had some rather large gaps. "But then how did you even know Mulvern House had an opening for a butler, or to list the Misses Piedmont as a reference?"

"One of our stagehands was a footman for the Misses Piedmont and told us all about them. They are two eccentric elderly sisters who never open the post for fear that the envelopes will contain bills. Tradesmen from the village have to call in person for payment. The sisters let their correspondence pile up on a table in the hall, then have the servants use them as kindling for the fires. I felt it was fairly safe to assume they wouldn't reply to an inquiry from an agency." As he spoke, his refined accent was slipping, his pronunciation drifting into a more relaxed cadence that indicated his modest background.

"Didn't the agency follow up when they didn't receive a reply?" Jasper asked.

The mischievous glint in Boggs's eye faded. "Perhaps I provided an incentive for the agency to overlook certain—er—gaps in my background. That's the only truly wrong thing I did," he added quickly, "and I do feel bad about that, but fewer and fewer people want to go into service nowadays. A trained butler is difficult to find, so it wasn't too hard to convince the agency to look the other way."

Jasper said, "Goodness, you're a brave chap—to go into service and aim for the top of the ladder."

"Well, sir, I supposed if I looked and acted like a distinguished butler and combined that with what my stagehand friend told me about how the Piedmont household ran, I thought I could do it. It couldn't be any harder than being on stage, and I'd have my own room and meals provided—at least that's what I thought."

His tone indicated he didn't think that any longer.

"But you've changed your mind?"

"Oh yes. Being on stage for a few hours every day is one thing. Being constantly in character is vastly different. A right strain, it is." The door opened and another waiter came out with a tray of drinks. Boggs spoke faster and inched toward the door. "I also knew you were asking questions about me, Miss Belgrave. I decided I'd had enough and made up the excuse to leave, but I've sent a letter to Lady Agnes with my resignation."

"And this is what you're doing now?" I gestured to the tray.

"I'm working with the catering company until something else opens up. I switched nights with another mate so I could be here. I knew this was an important evening for the family, and I wanted to make sure things went well." He put a hand to the door. "I must get back before I lose this job. I hope you'll keep my secret, Miss Belgrave?"

"Well, Lady Agnes already knows your real age, but she doesn't know about your background." I could certainly identify with being desperate enough to use unconventional means to land a job, and the fact that he'd wanted to be there that evening showed that although he wasn't a formally trained butler, he grasped the essence of the job. "I don't see any reason I'd mention anything about that to Lady Agnes or her brother."

"Thank you, Miss Belgrave," Boggs said, then gave us both a bow. "I hope you have an enjoyable evening." He pushed through the door.

"Well," Jasper said as we ambled back into the room, "that was generous of you, saying you wouldn't tattle on him about his background."

"What would be the point? He's not in the family's employment any longer. He didn't steal from them, and he's got another job—I know how hard it is to find employment. I'm certainly not about to sabotage him."

"Quite," Jasper said as he took two new glasses from a waiter who'd paused beside us. Jasper handed a glass to me. "Now before we were distracted, you were about to tell me what was on your mind."

I slowed my pace, picking my words as if I were making my way across a stream, stepping carefully from one exposed rock to another. "I have an idea. I've fit several pieces into a pattern that makes sense, but it's rather unbelievable—fantastic, even—and I haven't quite figured out the whole thing."

"What are the pieces—" Jasper broke off as a single voice carried above the hubbub.

"Gentlemen." Dennett's usually soft tones were gone, replaced with an exuberant bellow, and I wondered how many drinks he'd had before he arrived. He stood with a group of men. His cheeks and the tip of his nose were even brighter red than they'd been earlier. He held his champagne glass aloft."To digging in the Valley of the Kings."

A burst of conversation drowned out his next words. ". . . concession. I received news today from Dupin. He's withdrawn Mulvern's concession and given it to me."

One of the men clapped him on the shoulder. "Congratulations! May you be just as successful there as Lawrence was." He raised his glass, and the other men joined him in a toast.

Another man asked, "Will you continue digging in the same location as Mulvern?"

"He was a good excavator and found some nice pieces." He gestured to the plinth he stood beside, which held the large pot Lord Mulvern had reassembled. "But I don't think Mulvern had the larger picture in mind. I'll have to get in there and survey the whole place myself. I intend to go out just as soon as I can make arrangements."

My heart fluttered. I swiveled to Jasper and gripped his arm. "That's it—the last piece, and it fits perfectly," I said in a low voice.

A chime of silver against glass rang through the air, and conversation died down as everyone turned toward Lady Agnes. She'd stepped onto a small dais in one corner of the room, where a lectern had been set up. Beside her an easel held an oil painting of her uncle. Rathburn stood on the other side of the dais a few steps behind Lady Agnes.

"Later," I whispered to Jasper. Since Lady Agnes was about to speak, I couldn't have a whispered conversation with Jasper at the moment, but I was busily running through what I'd discovered and sorting out how I'd explain it to him—and Longly—as soon as her speech ended.

"Good evening, ladies and gentlemen." Lady Agnes's clear aristocratic tones carried across the room, and the remaining chitchat died away into silence. "Thank you for coming tonight to honor my uncle and all he's done in the field of Egyptology. I hope you enjoy looking at the beautiful antiquities we've curated here for you to view in this private opening event."

A round of applause followed this statement, and when the clapping faded, Lady Agnes went on, "I promise I won't take up too much of your evening with my boring soliloquy, but Gilbert and I did think it would be appropriate for us to take a moment and consider our uncle's work. He wasn't a professionally trained Egyptologist, but what he lacked in formal education, he made up for with enthusiastic study. Organizing this exhibit was one of his greatest desires. He wanted all Londoners to be able to see the beautiful artwork and sophisticated lifestyle of the Egyptians. The only touch of sadness tonight is that he's not here with us. Some of you will have heard that initially his death was thought to have been brought about by his own hand, but tonight I can assure you Uncle Lawrence didn't take his life—it was taken from him. In an unfortunate twist of fate, someone he trusted implicitly turned on him."

A rustling sound ran through the crowd, a low-level murmur, but I distinctly heard several people mentioned the name *Nunn*.

"But that's not true," I said. Lady Agnes had paused, and my words fell into that fragment of silence. Heads turned toward me. I'd spoken louder than I realized. Lady Agnes gave me a steely look from the lectern. "I'm afraid Miss Belgrave has a different point of view—"

"It's the correct point of view," I said with confidence. Interrupting a speech was terribly bad manners, but now that I'd put the pieces together, I knew exactly what had happened, and it wasn't right to blame Nunn.

"Oh, really?" Lady Agnes asked. "Would you care to explain that?" Sarcasm laced her tone.

My pulse thumped as I felt the weight of the crowd focusing on me. I'm sure she expected me to mumble an apology and fade into silence, but she'd handed me the perfect opportunity to trap the killer.

CHAPTER TWENTY-NINE

$\mathcal{I}$'d never been one to shy away when challenged, and this was too good of an opportunity to pass up, so I plunged in. Heart knocking in my chest, I set down my glass of champagne so no one could see how my hand was trembling. "Yes, I would like to explain. Thank you for the opportunity."

Someone gasped at my audacity, and whispers ran around the outer edge of the crowd. Jasper gave me a wink and said in a low voice, "Good luck, Miss Sherlock," as he took a step back, giving me the floor.

I cleared my throat and spoke over the murmurs and titters. "I've spent the last several days looking into the late Lord Mulvern's death. Lady Agnes herself was convinced that her uncle didn't commit suicide and wanted proof that he was murdered."

A buzz ran through the crowd. "Miss Belgrave, I must insist—" Lady Agnes began.

"I had a number of possible suspects," I said, raising my voice over hers and the hubbub. "The late Lord

Mulvern died after an evening dinner party at his home, and each person in attendance had the opportunity to slip away from the gathering and add extra sleeping powders to the tumbler he kept on his bedside table."

It's hard to resist a mystery, and I could feel the pull of curiosity as it tugged on the crowd. "Anyone who was at dinner that evening could have murdered Lord Mulvern, and almost everyone had a motive. Lord Mulvern's valet, Hodges, inherited a tidy sum on Lord Mulvern's death. The butler was new, and I uncovered some information that perhaps he wouldn't have wanted Lord Mulvern to know about." Boggs was moving through the crowd with a new tray of champagne flutes. His steps didn't slow, but he fixed his gaze on me as he navigated between the guests.

"Other members of the family had argued with Lord Mulvern about money and financial arrangements." My gaze skipped to Gilbert and Nora, who stood by the dais. Nora inched closer to Gilbert, and he put an arm around her shoulders. "Lord Mulvern's collection manager, Mr. Nunn, was at the dinner. Mr. Nunn knew his job was about to be eliminated, which gave him an excellent motive." I gestured to the dais. "Even Lady Agnes herself crossed my mind as a suspect."

Lady Agnes had turned and whispered to someone behind her, no doubt giving instructions to have someone escort me out of the gallery. She whipped back toward me with a look that scorched through the crowd. One woman near the dais actually took a step back.

I swallowed and pressed on, not sure how long I'd

have before I was removed. I'd already torched any bridge between Lady Agnes and myself. No use being circumspect now. "Perhaps Lady Agnes's request to investigate was a double bluff. With her uncle gone, her brother would most likely defer to her in all matters related to the Egyptian antiquities. She could run things as she liked."

Mumbles of agreement rippled around me. Everyone knew Lady Agnes managed Mulvern House and was the driving force related to their activities in Egypt. The flush in Lady Agnes's cheeks now rivaled Dennett's coloring.

I looked to Rathburn. "And Mr. Rathburn was also in attendance. Lord Mulvern was planning a donation to the museum. It would have been foolhardy for Mr. Rathburn to do anything to jeopardize the donation, but he was the only guest who I was able to confirm had slipped away from the dinner party and was alone for a period of time that evening."

Rathburn sputtered, but I hurried on, "Any one of these people could have murdered Lord Mulvern, but it was only tonight that I realized I was looking in the wrong place all along. The important question wasn't *who was at dinner*, but *who wasn't*. One person was desperate to get Lord Mulvern out of the way. The killer wasn't at the dinner that evening, but he *was* at Mulvern House." I turned and looked across the room. "Weren't you, Mr. Dennett?"

The crowd buzzed like a beehive that had been disturbed. "I don't know what you're talking about." Dennett sipped his champagne. "How could I have been in Mulvern House without anyone knowing?"

He looked so unconcerned that I felt a sinking inside. Was I wrong? Had I just made a fool of myself? I pressed down my doubts and poured conviction into my tone. I had to be right—it was the only answer that made sense. "You let yourself in with a key. Nora had left her handbag in a taxi the evening before. You had a copy of the key made, then had a friend return Nora's handbag, giving you a way to get in and out of Mulvern House undetected."

I took a few steps toward Dennett, my heels echoing in the room that had gone silent. Even the waiters had stopped circulating. Boggs stood immobile with his tray a few feet away from Dennett.

"The dinner hour is the perfect time to commit a murder, don't you think?" I said to Dennett. "In these days of reduced staff, everyone is required in the dining room or kitchen. There's no footman sitting on duty, waiting by the front door. He's in the dining room, waiting on the table. The family, staff, and guests are all gathered in the dining room, which gave you free run of the house. You were able to enter through the front door and go straight up the stairs. All you had to do was avoid Hodges, Lord Mulvern's valet. Once he'd finished preparing the room and retired below, you added the sleeping powders to the glass. Then you settled in to wait and make sure that they actually did the job. You couldn't set the scene with a suicide note until after Hodges attended Lord Mulvern after dinner. Once he left and Mulvern drank the Veronal and died, you could put out the suicide note."

By now the atmosphere in the gallery was charged. Everyone was riveted, their glances going from me to

Dennett, who swished his champagne flute through the air at me. "You're daft. Why would I do it? I had no reason to want Lord Mulvern dead."

"Didn't you? Everyone knows you're a bit obsessed with Egyptology. You're determined to dig in the Valley of the Kings. It's common knowledge you thought Lord Mulvern was digging in the wrong place. If only you were in charge, you'd be able to find a pharaoh's tomb. But Lord Mulvern never subscribed to your theories, did he?"

"More fool he. And I'll prove it next season."

"Yes, because now you have his concession."

Lady Agnes gasped. "But that concession stays within our family."

Dennett swung toward her. "Not any longer, Lady Agnes. Didn't Dupin contact you? He's withdrawn the concession from your family and given it to me. A perfectly legal transfer, I'll have you know," Dennett said.

"You came to a rather large inheritance recently, didn't you, Mr. Dennett?" I asked.

Dennett turned back to me. "What if I did? Uncle Elisha's death has nothing to do with this." He had a smile on his face as he shot glances at the men around him as if to say *let's humor the silly woman and let her continue to embarrass herself.*

"But it does. It gave you the ability to manipulate the officials in Egypt. Unfortunately, the top official was a friend of Lord Mulvern's. As long as Lord Mulvern was alive, you'd never get the concession you wanted. You couldn't dig in the exact spot where you *knew* treasures were buried. But with your inheritance, you now had money to bribe as many officials as you liked who could put pressure on Dupin to give you the concession. There was nothing in your way . . . except Lord Mulvern."

Dennett banged down his drink on a display cabinet and took a step toward me. His jovial smile had faded. Fear jolted through me at the hate in his gaze. Jasper shifted his stance, edging toward Dennett, but the crowd had pressed in around Jasper and there were several people between him and Dennett. "This is outrageous," Dennett said. "You can't prove a word of it."

My pulse jumped as he spit out the words. The atmosphere of the room changed. What had been an entertaining display, something to gossip about over tea tomorrow, had shifted to something ugly and dangerous. The other guests must have felt the hostility directed at me because they'd inched backward, clearing an open space between Dennett and me.

"Baseless accusations! Just theories," he said, spittle flying. "How could I hide in a house full of servants after dinner? That's impossible."

"Is it?" I asked, glancing around. If he charged at me, there were too many people to get away from him. I could snatch up my champagne and fling it at him, but that wasn't much of a defense. "There's an excellent place to hide within Lord Mulvern's room itself—the mummy coffin." Then I remembered the compact shaped like a gun in my evening bag. It might buy me a moment or two. "When I saw you standing in front of the row of coffins tonight, I realized the mummy coffin was the perfect place to hide."

As everyone glanced at the coffins lining the room, I unfastened the clasp of my handbag and inched my hand inside it. "The coffin in Lord Mulvern's room was positioned upright. All you had to do was slip inside for a couple hours and wait until Lord Mulvern awoke during the night and drank out of his tumbler. After he became drowsy, I imagine you added more sleeping powders to his tumbler and forced it down his throat. Then you set the stage with a suicide note, and that's where you had a stroke of good luck. I'm sure you came prepared with a forged note, but then you saw a discarded note in the wastepaper bin. It was in Lord Mulvern's own handwriting. All you had to do was snip off the top line and add a few characters to the scribbled words and you were all set. Once the note was on the desk, you let yourself out of the house without being seen and locked the door with your key."

"I won't stand for this any longer. It's absurd!" The flush on his cheeks had deepened to an angry red, and his chest heaved against the boiled shirt of his evening suit.

"Is it? Then why were your fingerprints inside the mummy coffin?"

"Impossible! I wore gloves—"

Dennett realized his mistake and charged. I yanked the compact shaped like a gun out of my handbag and leveled it at Dennett. A woman beside me shrieked and stumbled backward.

Dennett jerked to a stop, but he flexed his fingers as if in anticipation of getting them around my neck. His gaze cut to the door, then back to me.

"Don't move, Mr. Dennett. I'm sure the authorities

will be along shortly, and they'll want to speak to you." After Lady Agnes's quiet word to someone behind the lectern, I was surprised a museum employee or a police bobby hadn't appeared and escorted me out of the room already. "Perhaps Mr. Rathburn can round up a few guards to escort you out of here and wait with you until the police arrive."

No one moved. Rathburn still stood on the dais and was in my line of sight beyond Dennett's shoulder. I tilted my head at the door as I said, "Mr. Rathburn?"

"Oh, right. Certainly. That can be—er—arranged." Rathburn stepped down from the dais and waddled toward the door, but he was moving at such a ponderous rate it would be several minutes before anyone arrived to restrain Dennett.

Dennett squinted at the gun in my hand, and then he smiled in a way that made me go cold all over. Dennett gave a little flick of his hand toward his brow as if he were tipping his hat. "Excellent try, Miss Belgrave, but never bluff unless you're actually willing to follow through."

He spun around and shoved the plinth that held the large reassembled pot, then darted through the crowd in the opposite direction as the pottery rocked. A collective gasp went through the crowd as the pot wobbled, tilted, and fell. Boggs dropped his tray. Glasses splintered and champagne spattered as he stepped forward and caught the pot, cradling it against his chest like an oversized baby. I would have sighed with relief, but I'd already swiveled around and spotted Dennett pressing through the far edge of the crowd.

Then I saw Jasper's fair head moving through the

crowd at such a rapid pace that I blinked. Yes, it *was* Jasper. He rarely came out of his laconic state, but now he was sprinting to the door of the gallery. For a second I thought he was going to intercept Dennett, but his angle was wrong.

Jasper reached the door before Dennett and sprinted through it. Dennett reached it seconds later as the banner outside the gallery descended. Dennett ran directly into it like a sprinter breaking the tape at the finish line, except there was no breaking through the huge fabric banner, which tangled around him as he fought to bat it away.

Jasper sauntered into view and looped the cord that had held the banner up around Dennett a few times. Jasper tightened the cord, and the roll of fabric with Dennett inside teetered then fell. Jasper planted his foot on the writhing bundle.

I charged across the room to the door, and it took me a few seconds to realize why people were scattering out of my way. I still held the gun compact.

"It's fine. It's not really a gun," I said, and a lady in my path fainted, crumpling into her escort's arms.

I shoved the compact back into my handbag as I joined Jasper. He'd stepped back. Rathburn had returned and was directing several men to lift up the swaddled figure and carry it to an empty storage room. "Lock him in and stand guard until the police arrive," Rathburn instructed them.

"That's rather appropriate, don't you think?" Jasper said with a nod at the men hauling Dennett away. A section of his fair hair had fallen across his forehead, but otherwise he still looked perfectly groomed, not as if he'd just singlehandedly captured a fleeing murderer. "He hid in a mummy coffin to commit a crime, and now he's wrapped up like a mummy."

"Yes, very fitting," I said. "I'm sure Inspector Longly will appreciate the parallel."

"No doubt." Jasper turned back to me, his expression as serious as the time I fell out of the tree at Parkview and broke my arm. "You gave me quite a fright, waving that compact around. It was meant to deter crime—warn criminals off—not confront them."

"But that's exactly what I used it for, to keep Dennett away. It wasn't a hold-up, you know."

"I suppose that's true," Jasper said, and I noticed a tremor in his hands as he adjusted his tie and straightened his cuffs. "But what if Dennett had a gun as well—a real gun? What would you have done?"

"Thrown mine at him, I suppose. It doesn't matter now, does it? I'm fine. You saved the day with some quick thinking when you brought the banner down on Dennett." I forgot myself enough to brush his hair off his forehead, and his expression shifted, sending my heart back into flutters worse than I'd experienced a few moments before. I struggled to remember what I'd been about to say. "And—um—Boggs, yes, Boggs saved Lord Mulvern's pot from becoming a million tiny pieces again. It all played out beautifully, just as I expected."

Jasper laughed. "I don't believe that for a moment. Go on, admit it—you had no idea how it would end."

"All right. No, I didn't, but it was too good of an opportunity to pass up. I thought I could trip Mr. Dennett up, which was essential since I didn't have any proof of what he'd done."

"And you got him," Jasper said. "Good show, Olive. Well done."

I felt myself blush at his praise. Yes, that was definitely why I felt flushed. I said quickly, "But you caught him. Pulling the banner down on him was brilliant."

"I couldn't let him escape. Wouldn't be cricket, you know, but I certainly didn't want to have to do a rugby tackle. Far too fatiguing."

CHAPTER THIRTY

A few days later, I was walking around Mulvern Square as the first snowflakes of the season drifted down. I adjusted the wool scarf that Mrs. Hodges had given to me when I'd returned to inform Hodges of the outcome of my investigation. He'd been interested to hear the resolution and said, "I always did think there was something a bit too intense about that Mr. Dennett, if you know what I mean."

Thinking of Dennett's burning gaze that evening at the gallery opening, I quite agreed. Before I'd left, Mr. Hodges had presented me with a box. It contained the pale blue wool that I'd given to his mother on my last visit. "A little something from mother. It might be a trifle—um—long."

It was indeed the longest scarf I owned, but on a day like that one, the extra length was welcome, and I'd wrapped it twice around my throat.

I turned the corner at the park and spotted a familiar

figure coming my direction. It was Boggs, dressed in his bowler hat and a brown suit. I waved, and he crossed the street. "Miss Belgrave, how are you?" He raised his hat as he spoke.

"Very well. Have you been to visit Mulvern House?"

"Indeed I have. Thanks to the word you had with Lady Agnes, she doesn't have any hard feelings toward me about my little . . . stretching of the truth."

"I have to say it probably has more to do with your saving the Egyptian pot from smashing on the floor than anything I said."

"Perhaps, but thank you again, Miss Belgrave."

"I'm glad it worked out." We said our goodbyes and parted. I was a few steps down the street when I turned and called, "Boggs!"

"Yes, miss?"

"It occurs to me that you might be a useful person for me to know in my line of work. You're a dab hand at makeup and costumes too, I imagine. Plus, you're able to play different parts. If I should like to get in touch with you in a professional capacity, would you be interested?"

"Yes, miss. I would be. Very interested indeed." He named an address in Soho where he was staying, then said, "But I may not be there long. I have an audition for a gangster in a new play. You can always get in touch with me through my brother at the antique shop. He'll forward a message to me."

"Very well. I'll do it if I have need of you."

I continued on to Mulvern House and gave the new butler a thorough examination on entering the house.

As far as I could tell, his bald head was authentic and not a disguise. His bland expression, rather portly figure, and the stately pace he set as I followed him indicated he was just what he seemed—a butler through and through. I followed him up the red runner on the stairs to the drawing room, where he announced me.

Lady Agnes stood and crossed the room. The last time I'd seen her was at the end of the evening after the police had escorted Dennett out of the museum. I'd explained that I'd spoken to Boggs earlier and that he'd requested to work the exhibit opening because he knew it was an important event for the family. By then, Lady Agnes's anger toward me had cooled. She'd been cordial, but I certainly wouldn't have said we were on friendly terms. I wasn't sure what my reception would be today. I hoped she hadn't invited me to tea to give me a dressing down.

"Miss Belgrave, so glad you could join me for tea this afternoon," she said, and I was relieved she didn't have the tight, angry expression on her face that I'd seen when she was behind the lectern. Today, her friendly smile reminded me of the day I'd arrived at Mulvern House, when she'd been intent to recruit me to look into her uncle's death.

"It's my pleasure," I said.

"Perhaps you can give us your opinion," Lady Agnes said as she led the way across the room and gestured to a seat for me across from Nora, who said hello as she rolled a set of blueprints into a tube.

Lady Agnes said, "Don't put those away yet. Let's

get Miss Belgrave's opinion on the renovation possibilities." Nora unfurled the blueprints, and Lady Agnes said, "We have several options for the expansion."

"An expansion?" I asked. The town house was already a truly spacious home. I couldn't imagine they needed more room.

"Oh, not for us," Lady Agnes said.

"Of course not," Nora said. "It's for the antiquities, as it always is in this house." The words themselves could have been taken as a criticism, but she'd spoken with a lightness in her tone as if she was letting me in on a family joke.

"Nora's right," Lady Agnes said. "We certainly don't need more bedrooms. One option is to take in the bedrooms in the east wing and connect it to the grand gallery. Or we could extend the grand gallery so we can move the rest of Uncle Lawrence's collection out of storage."

We spent the next few minutes flipping back and forth between the blueprints and discussing the merits and drawbacks of both plans. The tea arrived, and Lady Agnes poured for us. A flash of movement in the hall caught my eye. Nora must have seen it too. She sat up a little bit straighter and called, "Gilbert, was that you?"

Gilbert poked his head around the doorframe. "Yes, I've returned. I'll join you in a moment."

"Nonsense," Nora said. "Come in and have your tea now while it's hot."

"It won't take a moment—"

"No, I insist. I'm pouring you a cup now. Cook sent up the ginger cookies you like so much. Do come in."

Gilbert hesitated a moment, and Nora frowned.

"Oh, all right," Gilbert said as he entered the room with a box under his arm. He'd used the doorframe to keep it out of sight. Nora clapped her hands. "Oh, a present. For me?" she asked with no trace of doubt.

"Of course it's for you, darling." Gilbert set the box in her lap and picked up his teacup.

Nora untied the ribbons and flicked off the lid. The cream and brown face of a Siamese cat popped up, its blue eyes darting back and forth. "A kitten," Nora breathed.

The cat climbed out of the box and poured itself into Nora's lap. A pink bow was tied to the collar. Nora stroked the kitten's back where the pale fur was barely darker than the snow flakes falling outside. "Aren't you lovely? What will Lapis think of you?" Nora glanced at Lady Agnes. "You won't mind having another cat, will you?"

"What? Ah . . . no. Not at all." Lady Agnes gave Gilbert a significant look.

He cleared his throat. "Nora, I thought the kitten would be good for us. We'll need some company in our new flat."

Nora's hand stopped moving. She twisted around to look Gilbert full in the face. "Our flat?"

Gilbert sat down on the sofa beside her. "It's an idea Aggie and I came up with. The town house is a perfect setting for a museum—The Mulvern Collection. Aggie would like to stay here and manage it. If we move out and Aggie moves to the east wing, that will free up the west wing, which will be plenty of room to display all of Uncle Lawrence's artifacts. I found a small flat on the other side of Hyde Park. What do you think of the idea?"

"What do I think? I think it's marvelous. I won't have to live in the same house with mummies. We'll have our own home with our very own kitty," she said, her voice taking on a squeaky tone. "Won't we, kitty?"

The kitten padded over to Gilbert, jumped up and arranged itself so it was draped over his shoulder. "I've got a head start with this one," he said as he rubbed the kitten's ears. "I think she might be my cat."

"We'll see about that," Nora said.

Lapis trotted through the door, paused, then moved stealthily across the room. The kitten and Lapis eyed each other. Gilbert transferred the kitten to the carpet. Within seconds, they were bounding around the room, a blur of pale fur. After a few rounds, Lapis hopped up onto the windowsill, and the kitten disappeared under the sofa.

Nora found a bit of fringe that had come loose from one of the pillows and kneeled on the floor to draw the kitten out. A few moments later, Gilbert joined her and dragged the ribbon from the box across the floor. A tiny paw emerged and stamped on the ribbon as Gilbert tugged it.

"More tea?" Lady Agnes asked me.

"No, thank you. I should be going."

Lady Agnes set the teapot down. "Before you go." She lowered her voice. "While Gilbert and Nora are occupied, I have to tell you how grateful I am for your help. I've realized I was a bit . . . hasty in my assessment of Mr. Nunn. I can see that now. You kept at it until the real culprit was caught. I appreciate that."

"It's a flaw I have. I'm afraid I'm dreadfully curious and can't rest until I know the truth."

"Well, I'm glad you didn't follow my directive. The outcome is still a sad situation with Mr. Dennett going to trial, but at least now we know exactly what happened."

"Honestly, I was surprised he confessed."

"Apparently, once the police found the copy of the key in his flat, he knew it was over. At least that's what Inspector Longly told me. He was quite nice. He called and explained about the key and Dennett's confession. I do have a question for you about the letter Mr. Dennett appropriated for the suicide note—how did you figure out what he'd done?"

I described how I'd discovered the suicide note was smaller than the writing paper in the desk. "It seemed odd that your uncle would trim a narrow section off the top of his suicide note. I thought the suicide note was probably a draft that Lord Mulvern had discarded because he wasn't happy with the wording or his penmanship. I wonder if they ever found the real letter. I imagine it was posted."

"Oh, they did," Lady Agnes said. "Inspector Longly told me about that too. Uncle Lawrence had written to one of his friends who edits an archaeological magazine. He'd invited Uncle Lawrence to contribute an article, but Uncle Lawrence declined, saying he couldn't because 'the Horus' was taking up all his time, meaning the paper he was writing about the various names and epithets associated with Horus. The first line read something along the lines of, 'Thank you for your kind invitation to contribute to the journal. I'd like to be included in the esteemed publication,' which was the part Mr. Dennett cut off. The next line read, 'I'm terribly sorry I cannot. The Horus prevents me.' There was just enough space for Mr. Dennett to extend the last stroke of the letter of the word *cannot* to cover up the period. Then he squeezed in the words *go on*. Inspector Longly said when they examined the paper under a microscope, it was possible to see where one bar in the capital *H* in the word *Horus* had been scratched away, probably with the scissors. The paper was so thick it didn't tear, and Inspector Thorn completely overlooked it. A few more carefully placed stokes made it possible that the word *Horus* could be mistaken for the word *horrors* because Uncle Lawrence's penmanship was so poor."

"It was quite clever," I said.

"But incredibly devious, which sums up Mr. Dennett," Lady Agnes said. "I find it hard to believe Mr. Dennett went from having tea here in this very room to stalking Mr. Nunn, watching for a moment when he could shove him into traffic. Then he went home, wrote Mr. Nunn's supposed suicide note, and posted it."

"Inspector Longly told you about the difference in the signatures?" I asked.

"He did." Lady Agnes's eyebrows wrinkled. "That was the flaw in Mr. Dennett's plan. Surely he realized the handwriting would be checked?"

"Perhaps he thought Inspector Thorn would be in charge of the investigation and wouldn't examine the suicide note too closely," I said. "So it must have been Mr. Dennett who planted the heart scarab in Mr. Nunn's room, which means it was Mr. Dennett who broke in and stole the amulets from the Zozar mummy."

Lady Agnes nodded. "Yes, Mr. Dennett said he'd see himself out, but instead of leaving, he slipped upstairs and hid the amulets in Mr. Nunn's room to make him appear to be dishonest. You're correct that Mr. Dennett was behind the theft of the amulets, but he didn't break into our house himself. He hired a thief to actually steal the amulets. Inspector Longly tracked down the man, who said Mr. Dennett had explained exactly where to look in the mummy wrappings." Lady Agnes pressed her lips together. "It makes me angry when I think about it. Such a waste, simply to satisfy his curiosity. Mr. Dennett couldn't stand knowing there were amulets within the wrapping and he couldn't have them. It sounds rather childish except that it was only a small manifestation of his obsession."

"Which extended to your uncle's concession," I said.

"I'm still surprised Mr. Dennett managed to convince Monsieur Dupin that we didn't want the concession any longer," Lady Agnes said, her gaze following Lapis and the kitten. She and Lapis were tearing around the room again as Gilbert and Nora watched them.

Lady Agnes went on, "Mr. Dennett scattered enough money around so that some of the less ethical officials persuaded Monsieur Dupin it was in the best interest of the Antiquities Service to grant the concession to Mr. Dennett. You were exactly right about Mr. Nunn being a scapegoat. Mr. Dennett must have realized you were close to uncovering the truth about Uncle Lawrence's death—that it wasn't suicide—so he set up Mr. Nunn to take the blame. Mr. Dennett had to give up the heart scarab he'd had stolen to throw suspicion on Mr. Nunn, but I suppose Mr. Dennett felt that was a small price to pay to make sure he wasn't implicated in Uncle Lawrence's death. Thank goodness I let Lapis's opinion of Mr. Dennett influence me. Otherwise, I might have allowed myself to become close to a murderer." Lady Agnes gave a little shake of her head. "But that's all in the past now and dealt with, thanks to you."

I was glad Lady Agnes appreciated what I had done, but I was uncomfortable with the praise. "Only one thing hasn't been cleared up. I wonder who left the note of hieroglyphic curses—um, I mean *warnings*—on my dressing table."

A crash sounded. A delicate piecrust table had toppled over, scattering books and magazines. Lapis and the kitten shot away, Lapis to her perch on the windowsill and the kitten to the underside of the sofa. Gilbert jumped up and righted the table. "Sorry, Aggie."

Lady Agnes crossed the room and picked up the books. "It's all right. None of the bindings are broken."

"I did," said a low voice at my elbow.

I looked down to Nora, who was still seated on the floor. "What?"

"I put the note on your dressing table." She pleated the pink ribbon and hurried on in muted tones. "I was so worried you'd find out Gilbert had been in Uncle Lawrence's room or uncover that it was me giving those stories to the newspaper. I knew you'd ask someone to tell you what it said, and I thought it might . . . I don't know . . . encourage you to give it up. I'm terribly sorry if it disturbed you."

"I didn't know you read hieroglyphics."

"Oh, I don't, but the library has endless shelves of boring tomes about Egypt. I just picked one at random and used the index to find what I needed. I copied it out exactly from the book."

How silly I'd been. I'd thought it could have been anyone except Nora. I'd completely overlooked the fact that everyone in Mulvern House had an extensive library dedicated to Egyptology at their disposal. I'd just never considered that Nora would go to the trouble to consult a scholarly book.

Gilbert and Lady Agnes had set the table to rights and were coming back across the room as Nora whispered, "Again, I'm terribly sorry if I gave you a fright."

"Well," Lady Agnes said as she took a seat across from me. "What were we discussing?"

I felt Nora's worried gaze on me. A few words would remind Lady Agnes of the topic we'd dropped, but I hated to ruin the new harmony in their household . . . and it couldn't hurt to have a woman like Nora in my debt.

I gave Nora a reassuring smile and said to Lady Agnes, "Whether or not you plan to return to Egypt after the collection here is open to the public."

"Of course," she replied immediately. "Egypt is in my blood. I'll always return there."

~

The snowflakes were spinning down faster and piling up at the edges of the pavement as I returned to Mrs. Gutler's. I bought a newspaper, happy to see Essie's story debunking the mummy's curse—a multi-part series—was on the front page, not buried in the back between engagements and weddings. I tucked the newspaper under my arm to read when I arrived at my room.

Lady Agnes's words echoed in my head as I walked along. She knew where she felt most at home and longed to return there, but I didn't have that. I didn't feel that way about Mrs. Gutler's boardinghouse. It was a temporary place. I was alighting there for the moment, but I certainly didn't intend to stay on forever. Sonia had taken over Tate House, and Nether Woodsmoor, while still a charming village, wasn't a comfortable place for me either. I loved Parkview, and I knew I would always be welcome, but it wasn't a place of my own. Perhaps one day I'd have a flat of my own or a cozy little house.

I shook the moisture off my coat, wiped my feet, and went inside the boardinghouse. I climbed the stairs to the top floor, unwinding the long blue scarf. Mrs. Gutler had slid the day's post under my door. A white envelope with Gwen's handwriting lay among the mail. The thick pure-white paper looked almost exotic next to the other cheap envelopes.

It contained an invitation to a party to celebrate their return from the continent. Gwen had enclosed a short note.

Dear Olive,

I hope you'll forgive us for not calling on you when we returned from Paris. We didn't even spend one night in London. Violet found this a great tragedy. I only regretted it because I couldn't call on you. Mother was determined to get to Parkview as soon as we possibly could.

Fortunately, I have an excuse to draw you back to Parkview straightaway. Do say you'll come to the party. I have so much to tell you. Violet had an invitation sent to Inspector Longly. Mother was awfully upset when she learned of it, but he's from a very good family and a childhood friend of Captain Inglebrook, whom we met in Monte. Captain Inglebrook is simply top drawer, so Mother couldn't grumble too much. I hope he—Inspector Longly—doesn't think the invitation too terribly forward. What if he thinks I made sure he received an invitation? What if he turns it down? What if he accepts? I don't know which is worse. Oh, come back to Parkview, Olive. I'll never make it through this party without you.

Your nervous cousin,
Gwen

P.S. We ordered some truly lovely frocks, including a purple one for you. I know you'll look absolutely smashing in it.

"Oh my," I said and sat down to pen an acceptance. Gwen sounded almost giddy. Gwen was never giddy—

that was Violet's department. I definitely had to return to Parkview.

Thank you for reading *The Egyptian Antiquities Murder*! Sign up for Sara's Notes and News Updates at SaraRosett.com/signup to get exclusive news, content, and giveaways.

THE STORY BEHIND THE STORY

*T*hank you for reading *The Egyptian Antiquities Murder!* This book grew out of my love of reading Elizabeth Peter's Amelia Peabody books. When I wrote the first book of the series, *Murder at Archly Manor,* I intentionally set it in 1923 so I could explore the fascination with all things Egyptian that gripped Europe after the discovery of King Tut's tomb in November of 1922.

People have always found Egypt intriguing. Ancient Greeks and Romans were early tourists and traveled to Egypt. Napoleon mounted a campaign to capture Egypt and took along a group of scholars to study and document the land. When Howard Carter's team uncovered a set of stairs in 1922 that led to the sealed tomb of a little-known boy pharaoh, it was just the most recent wave of Egyptomania—Tutmania.

The burial chamber was opened in February of 1923, and the amazing finds influenced art, architecture, fashion, and entertainment. Egyptian motifs and themes cropped up in movies, music, dress, and cosmetics. Even crime writers of the day were drawn to the subject. I was reading the archives of *The Sketch* on the British Newspaper Archive when I ran across the first publication of Agatha Christie's short story *The Adventure of the Egyptian Tomb* under the heading *The Grey Cells of M. Poirot* in the September 26, 1923 edition.

While researching the supposed victims of King Tut's curse, I read about Lord Westbury, a peer who jumped from the seventh-floor window of his London flat and died. The newspapers reported Lord Westbury was despondent after the death of his son, who had worked as a secretary to Howard Carter. Lord Westbury left a barely legible letter that stated, "I really can't stand any more horrors." The news articles were quick to point out the connection to King Tut and play up the curse angle. The death even made news in America. The *Gettysburg Times* of February 22, 1930 pointed out that in the years since the tomb had been discovered, there had been eight deaths of people "more or less intimately connected" to the tomb excavation, and most of those people had died sudden or violent deaths. Lord Westbury's death was the ninth. Although Lord Westbury's death occurred in 1930, I decided it would make an intriguing jumping off point for the fictional murder in *The Egyptian Antiquities Murder*.

Once I had the gist of the murder, I needed a setting and modeled my fictional Mulvern House on The Wallace Collection, a museum I was able to visit and highly recommend if you're in London. It's located at Hertford House in Manchester Square and houses an extensive collection of paintings, furniture, ceramics, sculpture, and armor. The house itself is gorgeous too! You can see images of The Wallace Collection on my Pinterest board dedicated to *The Egyptian Antiquities Murder* along with Olive's "gun" compact. Compacts' shapes went far beyond the basic round or square styles. There's also plenty of beautiful "frocks" as Olive would say on the board as well.

Monsieur Pierre Dupin is a fictional character I made up and wasn't in charge of granting archeologists the right to dig in Egypt. In reality, that person was Pierre Lacau. He was the director general of the Department of Antiquities of Egypt in 1923. He and Howard Carter didn't always see eye to eye.

Albert Rathburn didn't exist either, but I based his character on Sir E. A. Wallis Budge, who worked for the British Museum and made many trips to Egypt, where he bought antiquities from local dealers for the museum. All the large European museums wanted antiquities for their collections, and there was a race to acquire as many as possible. The methods used to procure the antiques were often questionable. The story Rathburn relates at dinner about tunneling underground from the Luxor Hotel to a nearby house to get a valuable papyrus was one of Budge's real-life experiences, which was recounted in Brian Fagan's book *The Rape of the Nile: Tomb Robbers, Tourists, and Archaeologists in Egypt* as well as in Wallis' own book, *By Nile and Tigris: A Narrative of Journeys in Egypt and Mesopotamia on behalf of the British Museum between the years of 1886 and 1913*. Wallis' book is available online at the Internet Archive. Fagan's book is a fascinating read if you want more details on how so many statues, obelisks, and mummies ended up in Europe.

If you'd like to know about new books from me, my personal book recommendations, and exclusive members-only book giveaways, sign up for my updates at SaraRosett.com/signup. Thanks again for going on this reading journey with me. I hope the book gave you a fun escape as well as a good mystery puzzle!

ABOUT THE AUTHOR

USA Today and Audible bestselling author Sara Rosett writes fun mysteries. Her books are light-hearted escapes for readers who enjoy interesting settings, quirky characters, and puzzling mysteries. *Publishers Weekly* called Sara's books, "satisfying," "well-executed," and "sparkling."

Sara loves to get new stamps in her passport and considers dark chocolate a daily requirement. Find out more at SaraRosett.com.

Connect with Sara
www.SaraRosett.com

ALSO BY SARA ROSETT

This is Sara Rosett's complete library at the time of
publication, but Sara has new books coming out all the time.
Sign up for her updates at SaraRosett.com/signup to stay up
to date on new releases.

High Society Lady Detective

Murder at Archly Manor

Murder at Blackburn Hall

The Egyptian Antiquities Murder

Murder in Black Tie

Murder on Location

Death in the English Countryside

Death in an English Cottage

Death in a Stately Home

Death in an Elegant City

Menace at the Christmas Market (novella)

Death in an English Garden

Death at an English Wedding

On the Run

Elusive

Secretive